# A Place Called

# Winter

A novel by

## JUDITH KELLY QUAEMPTS

A Place Called Winter

Copyright © 2014 by Judith Kelly Quaempts

Cover image by Eric James Quaempts

# A Place Called Winter

This book is dedicated to the best parents anyone
could hope for:

John Joseph Kelly (Sept. 1918-Feb. 2009)
Clare Gianelli Kelly (June 1921-July 2006)

and to

Joan Kelly Phillips and Diane Kelly,
sisters extraordinaire

# PROLOGUE

The flickering light above the motel room throws her face into shadow. He feels her hesitation when he reaches in front of her to open the door.

"What's wrong, change of heart?" His voice is gentle. Women like gentle. They trust it.

She shakes her head. "I haven't changed my mind. I should call home, though, and tell my son I'll be late."

"No problem. While you make your call I'll pour us a drink."

He opens the door, places his hand on the small of her back, and guides her inside.

A low wattage lamp lends a benign glow, softening the effect of the cigarette burned carpet, threadbare furniture, and bedspread faded beyond color. A strip of torn wallpaper and the spreading water stain above it are just two more shadows in the subdued light.

He points to the phone. While she dials he removes plastic wrap from two glasses on a scarred console. From his bag he takes a bottle of Makers Mark – he hates cheap whiskey – and pours two generous shots.

She whispers, "Good night," into the phone as he hands her a drink. She hangs up and her expression is curious, as though she can't understand what she's doing in this room with a man she met just hours ago. But she tosses the drink back and holds her glass out for more. He bends down and kisses her gently on the mouth, lets his lips linger until she returns the pressure. Then he takes the glass from her hand.

\*\*\*

Sweat, sex, and cheap perfume. The odors lie on the back of his throat like rancid butter. He lifts his head from the crook of her neck and stares into her wide blue eyes. Her blonde hair, ephemeral as a cloud earlier, looks like dry straw. A delicate chain of bruises darken her neck. He studies her parted lips, lips he kissed, sucked, and chewed until no trace of bright lipstick remained. A ruby bead glistens where his teeth nipped the tiniest bit too hard, and her mascara has bled into the parched skin around her eyes. She looks like a surprised raccoon, a surprised and very dead raccoon. He barks out a rueful laugh and with a groan, rolls off her flaccid belly. Cupping his sore privates, he heads for the shower.

After he dresses, he checks his pickup. The truck with its canopy shell is backed up to the door. He steps out and scans the parking lot. Nothing moves. No witnesses. He gathers her clothes and puts them into his overnight bag. His movements are unhurried, meticulous. Before he wraps her purse and body in the tarp taken from his pickup, he removes one of her earrings. He makes two trips, carrying her out first, sliding her into the bed under the canopy, returning to the room for one last look around before grabbing his bag. In a few hours an overworked, underpaid maid will strip the bed, wash the shower and sink with bleach, collect the glasses for re-sanitizing, and pick up the two-dollar tip he left on the console. By then he'll be miles away while Doreen, Norene, whatever the hell her name was, will stay, weighted by rocks in the McKenzie River. The river rises and falls according to season and the rocks holding her down will eventually tumble away with the current and set her free, but that's no concern of his. By then, no trace of him will remain. His stomach growls as he exits the parking lot. He's suddenly ravenous. After he disposes of her, he'll stop for a good breakfast before hitting the freeway for home.

# 1

arol Ingram arrived for work fifteen minutes early, as she had every morning for the last ten years. At noon, she ate her lunch in the staff lounge, ignoring the silence that fell when she walked in, a silence fueled by rumor and innuendo; and maybe some pity, too. At five, she switched her phone over to voice mail, straightened the papers in her IN box, then stuck her head around the Dean's office door to say she'd see him tomorrow. On her way home, she drove up to a mailbox and posted her rent. At three a.m. the next morning, Carol stood in her dark apartment looking out the window. A full moon threw the landscape into bright relief and revealed no lurking shadows, no car idling across the street. The bushes along the walk were bushes, nothing more. Seconds later, carrying a single suitcase, she shut and locked the door behind her, walked to her car, and started the engine. She did not turn on the headlights until she was a block away.

Once she reached I-5 North, she drove in a near trance, measuring the miles she traveled by the cities she passed, cities with names like Colusa, Willows, Red Bluff, Yreka. The full moon appeared to lead her, a gold orb floating just beyond the hood of her car. When day broke, the moon remained bleached white as bone against the deepening sky. She lost sight of it when she crossed the border into Oregon. At Ashland, she exited for gas and went into the convenience store to use the restroom. She washed her hands and face, careful to avoid looking in the speckled mirror above the sink. On her way to the register, she picked up four bottles of water and a handful of energy bars. The cashier, a hard-looking woman with hair dyed an impossible shade of red, glanced up from her magazine. Her eyes widened; then dropped. She didn't raise them again, even to hand Carol her change.

Medford, Wolf Creek, Sutherlin, Cottage Grove; by the time she reached Eugene, Carol was stiff with exhaustion. She stopped again and bought a tall coffee from the kiosk inside the station while an attendant filled her tank. This time she kept her head down when she paid. She ran into heavy rain leaving Eugene. Truck tires threw sheets of water across her windshield, more than the wipers could handle. She drove, clenching the wheel, until the rain dwindled to a silver drizzle outside Portland. By the time she reached her exit, the skies were clear. The Columbia Gorge rejuvenated her. Red rock hills rose steeply above the wide river, pockets of mist floated over the water. Clouds came and went, playing tag with the sun. Occasional drops of gusty rain spattered her windshield; then disappeared in the brilliant sunlight that followed.

On the outskirts of Hood River, a siren wailed. A look in the rear view mirror revealed blue and white flashers speeding toward her. Carol barely had time to pull onto the shoulder before a state police car sped past, the shield on its door a blur of gold. She reached for a bottle of water, fingers shaking as she twisted the lid off. She had to hold the bottle with both hands to bring it to her mouth. When she pulled back onto the freeway, the siren still echoed inside her head. One hand drifted to the angry red whorls on her cheek and she forced it back onto the steering wheel. Three hours later, she stopped outside Pendleton, filled the tank again, and drove on, leaving 84 at the Mission interchange. She passed the United States Forest Service offices, a truck stop, the tribal Casino. At a four-way stop near the tribal governance center, she made a right turn onto a two-lane highway that took her through housing areas and by a clinic and Longhouse. Another turn, more miles, small enclaves named Cayuse, Thornhollow.

Thirty miles later, a sign: Welcome to Winter – Population 53.

She passed the old store, deserted when she was a kid, now sporting a fresh coat of white paint and a red-lettered OPEN sign in front. Then she crossed Sorrow Creek Bridge and turned onto a dirt lane marked by a black mailbox with Fuller stenciled on its side. The lane zigzagged for a quarter mile or so before disappearing behind a stand of trees. Beyond those trees the house waited.

Carol wrenched the steering wheel to the right, coasting over the grassy bank above Sorrow Creek, and stopped beneath a cottonwood tree. She cut the engine and climbed from the car. Twenty-two years since she last saw this place, but the air was the same, an intoxicating mix of pinesap, wet stones, and rotting leaves. She turned a slow circle, taking in the tree-studded hills, the tangle of blackberry vines in the meadow, the willows and alders that grew thick in the creek shallows. A red-tailed hawk drifted on thermals overhead. Unseen, quail chattered in the brush. Carol closed her eyes and let the sun bathe her face. A thin breeze lifted the new leaves on the cottonwood and set them whispering. A mourning dove's haunting cry drifted from the hillside. At last. Sanctuary.

# 2

Cedar-sided, silvered by summer heat and winter cold, the small, square house merged into the landscape so well it might have taken root there. Weather-speckled windows mirrored floating clouds. Spider webs, thick as cotton-candy, trembled beneath the porch eaves. Locust trees waved branches above the roof's eastern side. The weeping willow, leaves still greening, had grown huge in the years she'd been gone. Reality struck like a hammer blow. Carol's knees buckled. Until this moment, nothing had seemed real – the life left behind, the nearly nine-hundred-mile drive, an uncertain future. She grabbed the gatepost for support and waited for the dizziness to pass. Somewhere, a blue jay squawked. She raised her head, caught a flash of light halfway up the pine-studded ridge, and narrowed her gaze. Nothing. Her mind playing tricks after the long drive? She stepped through the gate on still-wobbly legs, and started up the path.

The key slid into the lock with ease. Carol bit her lip before she turned the knob.

Stale air, faintly scented with tobacco, met her. A sudden image: Uncle James, tapping tobacco onto a cigarette paper, a quick roll and lick to seal the edge, a twist for the end he would light.

For an impossible moment she expected to see him coming toward her, arms thrown wide in welcome as they had been all the years of her childhood.

But there would be no welcome. James was dead. All that greeted her now were motes of dust stirred by her entry, a small tornado of minute bits lit by late afternoon sunlight slanting through the windows.

Carol let out a sigh and gazed around. Little had changed. Bookcases still crammed with books on every subject. The 1940's sofa and armchair bought second-hand and refurbished, a little faded. The crocheted pad she'd made for him when she was eleven still cushioned the seat of his oak rocker. His Persian rug formed a pool of color against the red fir floor.

The only new thing in the room was a state-of-the-art CD player on the bookcase and the CD rack beside it. She crossed the room and ran her finger over the CDs: Peterson, Davis, Rachmaninov, Bach; some hard rock, a lot of blues. James' tastes had always been eclectic.

No television. Not surprising.

"A waste of time and a waste of mind," James used to say.

She yawned. Fifteen hours on the road taking their toll, and too many sleepless nights before that. The few things in the car could wait. Right now, the sofa beckoned.

She took off her shoes and curled into its softness, asleep before her head reached the cushion.

*\*\*\**

She woke with a start, disoriented. Shadows moved across the ceiling, light dappled a rug the color of gemstones. She sat up, ran a hand over her face, and winced when she hit a tender spot. She glanced at her watch, surprised. Only half an hour gone, yet she felt more rested now than she had in weeks.

Feeling safe. What a difference it made.

She got up and slipped into her shoes. Time she reacquainted herself with the rest of the house.

Her uncle had built the house with simple in mind. A generous living room and kitchen in front, bedroom, bath and utility set in back, divided by a short hallway. Stairs in the living room to a loft with a bedroom and bath built into the northeast corner – her old room.

In the kitchen, French doors framed a wood deck and side yard. The green soapstone counters were new, but the hand-crafted pine cupboards and pine table remained, the table situated so one could look outside while eating. How many times had she and James watched deer graze on the hillside while seated there?

Upstairs, she found the door to her bedroom closed. She opened it and fell straight back into her childhood.

Tall, unadorned windows. Who needed curtains with a view all sky and trees? Her bed, with its antique iron frame situated between north- and east-facing windows, a flea-market find her uncle sandblasted and repainted for her thirteenth birthday. Her grandmother's cedar chest sat at its foot. Carol kneeled and raised the lid. Twin scents of cedar and lavender rose from the neatly folded linens and quilts stored inside.

The closet held empty hangers. A faded Muriel cigar box peeked from the overhead shelf. Curious, Carol lifted it down and carried it to the bed. The cracked rubber bands holding the lid snapped as she eased them off. Inside were old photographs of her, alone, or with Rick and Lorrie and Will, or her parents. She smiled, seeing herself at ten, skinny and shapeless, braces glinting behind her wide smile. She stood in the creek, holding her first catch, a trout she later realized her uncle hooked before pretending disgust at his lack of luck and handing her the pole. Her smile faded when she came to one of her at fourteen, standing between her parents in front of James' house. How happy they looked. She closed the lid and returned the box to the shelf. She'd save the pictures for another time, when her emotions weren't so close to the surface.

Her uncle's bedroom she saved for last. His bed and clothes had been burned according to his wishes. What remained was his battered oak desk, the fly-tying vise still clamped to one edge. Three fishing rods and boxes of notebooks waited in the closet. Like the photographs, she would leave the notebooks shut away until she could handle looking through them. For the briefest of moments, Carol considered moving her bed here, but rejected the thought. She couldn't sleep in James' room. James wouldn't haunt her dreams, but her conscience might.

\*\*\*

Snack bars bought on her trip substituted for dinner. She washed them down with ice-cold well water smelling of sulfur. Then, wrapped in a blanket taken from the cedar chest, she went to the porch and watched the moon rise. Hard to believe this was the same moon that guided her from California. It looked so much bigger here. Lulled by the rustle of leaves and the croaking of frogs, she dozed until the hoot of an owl roused her. She took a last look at the moon and the dark silhouettes of the pines on the ridge before she went inside and made up her bed.

# 3

"Will! Wake up. For heaven's sake, have you been out here all night?"

A firm hand shook Will's shoulder. Something rough and wet lapped his fingers. He opened his eyes, saw Lady licking his hand. Luce stood over him in her red bathrobe, exasperation and amusement evident in her husky voice.

He ran his tongue over his lips and glanced at his watch. What the...? Seven? In the morning? He rubbed his face, feeling sandpaper stubble along his jaw.

"Coffee's made," Luce said, tightening the sash on her robe. "Go shower."

She left him knuckling his eyes. The last thing he remembered was the clock striking eleven. Luce said good night. Then...what?

Paper littered the end table beside his chair. He'd been in the living room, working on his accounts, a pencil and paper man despite the computer in his office. He'd heard Luce's low voice, visiting on the phone with a girlfriend in Portland. After she said good-night and went to her room, he dropped all pretense of working and laid his paperwork aside. Carol was back, so changed he'd hardly recognized her.

He'd been on the hillside, studying an eagle nest on the opposite ridge, when he heard a car coming down James' private road. When it stopped at the house, he'd swung the binoculars down in time to see a skinny kid with wild hair climb from the driver's seat and head for the gate. Trespasser or someone lost and in need of directions? Well, he wouldn't find them in an empty house. While Will watched, the kid stumbled, staggered, and grabbed for the gatepost. A pale face lifted in his direction. Shock kicked his pulse into overdrive. The binoculars slipped from his hands. No kid. No boy either. There was no mistaking the oddly colored, almond-shaped eyes, the auburn hair that had been hacked rather than cut. Her face!

Lady, curled at his side, whined. "It's okay," he'd murmured, dropping a comforting hand on her flank. But it wasn't okay. Carol. What in God's mercy had happened to her?

He still remembered the gawky, toothsome girl of eight, come to spend the summer with her uncle. Summer by summer she changed until at fifteen, she transformed into a lissome beauty. When had he realized his feelings, too, had changed, become more than brotherly? Images flashed through his mind: Carol at ten, wide-eyed with delight when he found a wind-downed bird's nest for her collection; Carol at twelve, her peal of triumphant laughter when she beat him at Scrabble. Then the moment at the river, his heart hammering as he put his arm around her, and she turned her face up to his, eyes wide and trusting.

Their kiss changed everything. When it ended, they broke apart, stunned.

First love. Amazing anyone survived it.

They'd been ecstatic that last summer, until she learned of her parents' coming divorce.

Until his stepfather found them together.

Will's hands clenched. His stepfather. Even dead, Ray brought instant rage.

Through the years, Carol remained a bittersweet memory, fifteen, forever beautiful. The woman framed in his binoculars yesterday – a gaunt caricature of that girl – pierced his heart.

"Here Will." Luce held a steaming cup of coffee under his nose. Her action ended his reverie. He got to his feet. "Thanks."

He gulped the hot brew on his way to the bathroom, set the cup aside, and lathered his face.

But instead of his reflection in the mirror, he saw Carol's, the look in her deep-water eyes that day at the creek, before everything went terribly wrong.

Goddammit, anyway.

\*\*\*

Luce waited at the door, holding a travel cup in one hand, a napkin-wrapped egg sandwich in the other.

"Call Milbank, would you please, Luce?" Will said. "Phone number's on the list. Let him know I'm running a little behind but on my way."

"Yeah, yeah." Luce placed both hands on her hips. "But I'm adding this to my raise request. Just because you're helping me out by giving me a place to stay doesn't mean you can take advantage, you know."

Will planted a grateful kiss on her forehead before hurrying out.

# 4

Light seeped through her closed lids. Carol turned over and burrowed deeper under the quilt, chasing the remnants of a technicolor dream.

A hideous shriek broke the silence. She bolted upright, clawing at air.

A woman's scream?

Another shriek came.

Her heart jumped to her throat. She slid from bed and hurried to the window.

The words burst from her. "I must be dreaming!"

Below, peacocks strutted through the yard. A male dragged his brilliant train through the dew-wet grass.

She blinked, rubbed her eyes, and looked again. They were real. Where on earth had they come from? Now fully awake, she glanced at her bedside clock. Seven. In the morning. She had slept the night through without the nightmares that had plagued her since the attack.

She looked back outside. Sunlight poured over the ridge thick as honey, creating rainbows in the wet grass. The peacocks were gone, most likely into the scrub brush at the base of the hill.

Carol leaned her head against the cool glass pane. How many hours had she spent dreaming in this room as a child? At eight she was a princess in the tower, waiting for rescue by one of King Arthur's knights. Later, she traded her royal robes for a pirate sword and led an all-male crew of cut throats. A different dream came at fifteen, only to become a recurring nightmare affecting the rest of her life.

Will.

She turned from the window and made the bed. The present was nightmare enough; no need to add the long ago past.

After a shower, Carol dressed in clothing wrinkled from hasty packing and headed downstairs. She missed her morning coffee and wondered how early the store opened. Standing by the French doors, a stealthy movement at the edge of the lawn caught her eye. She held her breath as a doe stepped gingerly into the yard and lowered her head to graze. Seconds later, two others joined her. A saying her mother was fond of popped into Carol's head: Today is the first day of the rest of your life. On a morning like this, she could almost believe it.

# 5

When Carol entered the store a cowbell jangled above the door. Classical music poured from speakers set in two corners near the ceiling. She had been inside once before, when it stood empty. She and Lorrie, twelve then, had climbed through a broken window and crept through the rooms until the shadows took on monster shapes and sent them back outside giggling and screaming.

Now, the once grimed floors gleamed. An antique oak cooler with glass doors held butter, milk, bricks of cheese and packaged lunch meats. Shelves on the opposite wall offered staples: bread, sugar, flour, coffee. Coffee. She wrinkled her nose. Not the brand she was used to, but when in Rome...

"Help you?"

Her hands flew to her face. She turned, taking a step back.

A silver-haired man with startling blue eyes stepped from a shadowed corner near the window.

"Ben Wagner," he said. "I'm sorry. I didn't mean to startle you."

The silver hair belied the youthful face beneath. He could be any age from thirty-five to fifty-five, Carol thought. Smile lines bracketed his mouth, fanned from the corners of his mesmerizing eyes.

"My fault," she stammered. "I didn't see you when I came in."

"You're James' niece."

She nodded. "How did you...?"

"Your eyes," he said. "Gray one minute, almost green the next. Just like his. I used to kid him they were the color of the water because he spent so much time on the river."

Carol smiled. "He loved to fish."

"We had that in common. James was a wonderful man, very much missed."

"Thank you."

"So, what brings you into my store?"

"Coffee." She nodded toward a tin on the shelf. "I'd kill for a good French roast, but I'll settle for that until I get to town."

"Well, today's your lucky day. The real thing is in my kitchen. On the house, a welcome to Winter, if you will. You take sugar or cream?"

"Just the way it comes, please."

He walked behind the counter and disappeared down a short hallway. Cutlery rattled, a cupboard door banged shut.

It struck her then. Ben Wagner hadn't even blinked when she turned to face him.

Carol picked up the tin of coffee along with two cans of vegetable soup and one of tuna. She set them on the counter as Ben reappeared.

Her nose twitched at the aroma of freshly brewed coffee.

"Here you go," he said.

"Thank you." Carol knew fine china when she saw it and this was the real McCoy, porcelain, translucent as spun air. Red poppies, gold buttercups, and celadon stems with graceful, half-furled leaves, bordered the rims of both cup and saucer.

"Good Lord, this is so beautiful I'm afraid to touch it."

He shook his head. "Don't be. I picked up an entire set for twelve at an estate sale for not much more than a plastic starter set at Wal-Mart."

Carol doubted it. More likely, he wanted to put her at ease.

Balancing the saucer in one hand, Carol grasped the delicate handle and brought the cup to her mouth.

"What happened to your face?"

Cursing her suddenly shaking hand, Carol set the cup back on its saucer.

Ben grimaced. "Christ, I'm sorry. I've offended you." He reached across the counter, his touch clumsy. "Please, forgive me. My mouth overrides my brain sometimes."

"That's okay," she said, avoiding his eyes. "I'm still getting used to it myself. Car accident. The window –"

The jangling bell cut short her lie. Ben's eyes shifted to the door.

"Lucinda," he said. "You're out early. Meet Carol Ingram, your new neighbor."

The woman stood inside the door, a sardonic smile on her perfectly made up lips. Blonde hair in styled disarray, skin tight jeans worn with a form fitting pink shirt, she was everything Carol was not, from her unblemished face to her manicured nails. Yet, behind that careful façade, Carol thought she saw a child lurking in the soft brown eyes that traveled from Ben to her and back again.

"This is Lucinda Frye," Ben continued. "Everyone calls her Luce. She and Will Jacobs live in Cora Newsome's old house."

Will? Here? Carol fought to keep her expression calm. "Hello," she said. "What beautiful earrings. Dream catchers, right?" She meant the compliment, though she thought the whole dream-catcher thing had grown overdone of late. Luce's appeared one-of-a-kind: delicate sterling silver webs spun by miniscule turquoise spiders with coral chip eyes.

A finger painted pale pink reached up and touched one earring. "Thanks. Will gave them to me for my birthday." She giggled, no longer a sophisticated woman but a delighted child. "I picked them out, though."

What a contrast we make. I'm surprised Ben didn't say, Beautiful Swan, meet Ugly Duckling, or better yet, Beauty meet Beast. "Well, I'd better pay for my things and get a move on," Carol said.

"You don't have to rush off," Ben said. "Have more coffee."

"I'll take some," Luce said, and before Ben could react, hurried behind the counter and down the hall.

Ben gave a rueful smile. "I don't know how Will keeps up with her."

Carol was reaching for the groceries when the sound of breaking china came. She looked at Ben. He rolled his eyes and raised them to the ceiling.

"Why me, Oh Lord," he whispered, looking so comical Carol almost laughed.

Luce reappeared clutching a saucer. "I'm so sorry, Ben. The cup is a total loss, but the saucer is fine. You can hardly see the crack."

"It's only a dish, Luce, not one of the crown jewels," Ben said. "I don't imagine I'll need to serve twelve coffees at once."

He took the saucer from Luce's hand and laid it on the counter. "Let me carry your things to the car, Carol."

They were at the door when he said, "Sorry, I forgot something. Back in a minute."

He wheeled around, her groceries still in his arm.

When he returned he apologized again. "Had to turn my oven off."

In the parking lot, Carol noticed peacock feathers on the ground and bent to pick a couple up. Ben opened her car door and set her groceries on the seat.

"My yard was filled with peacocks this morning," she said. "I thought I was dreaming." Absentmindedly, she smoothed one feather's ragged edge. "Actually, they scared me awake. I thought I heard a woman screaming."

"They're noisy damn birds at times," Ben said. "But Jackson loves them."

"Jackson?"

"Jackson Henry. He lives just this side of the bridge, back in the trees near the river. Moved here a couple of years ago." He toed the gravel with his shoe. "Jackson's a big guy, and I do mean big, something like six-ten big. He builds guitars – custom jobs – and raises peacocks on the side. The man likes his solitude, but then, we all do. Why else choose to live here?"

Ben nodded to a small bungalow across the road. "Of course, solitude can prove a hardship. Cora Newsome sold her place to Will after she broke her hip last winter. Pure luck I happened by to bring her groceries. She could have died from exposure. Living across from me, I'm able to keep an eye on her."

Carol leaned against the car. "I remember Cora. I was always a little afraid of her. I don't think she cared very much for us kids. Roger died?"

"No." Ben's mouth turned down. "He ran off with another woman long before I came on the scene. I don't think Cora ever recovered."

"That's sad."

"Yes," Ben said. "It is. Did you know Will, too?"

"I did."

When she failed to elaborate, Ben said, "Terrible thing, losing his wife like he did."

"His wife? But isn't Luce – "

His laugh cut off her question. "Heck, no. She and Will's mom were close. Way I heard it, Will is giving her a place to stay while she sorts through some problem or other." He flicked one of the feathers Carol held. "Are you keeping these?"

"No. Do you want them?"

"Sure, I use them for fly-tying. My mom used to keep the real colorful ones in a vase on the coffee table," Ben said, taking them from her hand. "Bought them at a flea market, I think." He shook his head. "Imagine paying for them. These, of course, are from the hens, not at all pretty, but good for making herl."

"Herl? That sounds familiar. Uncle James tied his own flies but I can't remember what herl was used for."

"Royal Coachman, for one," Ben said with a smile. He held a feather up, a far away look coming into his eyes. "Mom used to tickle our noses with those feathers sometimes."

"So, you have brothers and sisters?"

His brow furrowed. "No. What makes you ask?"

"You just said, 'she tickled our noses.' Didn't you mean –?"

"Oh," he said, his forehead smoothing out. "No. Only child. I was talking about my friends. Mom got a kick out of embarrassing me, I think."

Carol grinned. "I think it's a rule of motherhood. Mine liked to show my friends her dance moves." She glanced at her watch. "Yikes, I'd better get a move on. Thanks Ben, for the coffee."

"Come back soon, Carol. Coffee's always on."

# 6

Carol found the coffee beans when she put the groceries away. Ben had substituted his own for the tin when he claimed to be turning his oven off.

What a sweet man.

Uh-oh. Grinder. Had she seen one in the pantry? Yes. She brought it into the kitchen, plugged it in, and added the beans. Sweet Lord, what a wonderful smell!

She brewed a pot, filled an oversized mug, and took it to the table while she made out her list. The lawn needed mowing, the house needed washing down, and the entire inside needed a good dust-up. She considered switching utilities to her name and decided against it. She didn't want to scatter bread crumbs if Malone tried finding her. The companies wouldn't care whose name appeared on the checks as long as they got paid. As for mail, no reason to change that either. She hadn't left a forwarding address.

She found the mower under a tarp in the woodshed. Uncle James had left his lawn and garden tools in good condition and they hung aligned by size from mounted wall brackets. Coiled hoses slumbered like snakes beside an old wooden apple box containing various sprinkler heads and nozzles. The red gas container was full.

Carol added gas and oil to the empty reservoirs then rolled the mower onto the lawn. With a silent prayer to all lawn gods, she pulled the cord. The engine caught.

"I am woman, hear me roar," she sang and started forward over the grass.

For lunch, she ate tuna straight from the can standing at the kitchen sink. The scent of new-mown grass drifted through the open window, reminding her of childhood summers when she helped James in the yard and never considered it work.

By late afternoon, she'd hosed the exterior free of grime, washed the windows she could reach, and dusted and vacuumed all of inside. A blue glass vase on the coffee table held a spray of wild cherry. Sunlight danced off the walls and played on the lush colors of the rug.

Carol took a deep breath and let it out, contented with the day's work. Her eyes fell on a heron James carved from a cottonwood root and a memory stirred.

She snapped her fingers. Of course! How could she forget?

She hurried outside to the woodshed. The mural, though faded by time, remained as beautiful as the summer day James painted it. Sorrow Creek. A great blue heron standing in water so clear, every stone on the bottom shimmered with light, a silver ribbon of minnows swimming below the lucent surface. On the creek bank cottonwoods green against a summer sky where a red-tailed hawk soared on thermals. She had been twelve that summer. When James caught her watching him, he'd handed her a brush. The yellow and blue daubs in the foreground were hers: buttercups and bachelor buttons, the same wildflowers blooming in the meadows now. She reached out and traced their initials with her finger: jef/cmi – James Edward Fuller, Carol Michelle Ingram. Her eyes burned. All those happy hours. Her uncle had been the sun around which her small planet orbited, Winter her private universe.

At twelve she believed happiness lasted forever.

# 7

Over the next two weeks, Carol settled into a rhythm ruled by light. She woke to skies the color of old bone and drank coffee sitting on the front porch. She loved the early morning calm, the touch of cool air on her skin. Insects hummed, pines sung in breezes blowing down the ridge. Time had no meaning except to separate day from night. She took long walks, discovering plants she hadn't seen in years: yellow violets, Dutchmen's Britches, Lady Slippers growing through emerald beds of moss. Wild plum, cherry and apple trees were in bloom, their scent enough to drive a person wild.

She came upon these in such odd places she knew that only the birds could have done the planting. In the evenings she read her uncle's books, listened to his music, and sometimes simply sat letting the silence soak into her. If the crack of a tree branch made her start, or a moth batting against a dark window made her jump, she accepted it as part of the penance she must pay before she felt truly safe again. But each passing day loosened the stubborn knot of fear inside her. One day, that knot would unravel altogether.

Late afternoons brought her to the porch again to watch the sun set. As the light loosened its hold, nighthawks and bats arrived, swooping and darting to feast on insects that moved through the air like speckled clouds.

On one such afternoon, Carol sat waiting for the sun's alchemy to color the sky when she heard a car coming down her road. She fought an impulse to run and hide. He couldn't possibly have found her this soon. Her fingernails dug into her palms as a red Miata burst through the trees and sped toward her. The car braked near the gate, raising a cloud of dust. Doors on both sides flew open. Two people climbed out and hurried toward her.

She recognized them at once, took a steadying breath, and rose to greet them.

"Why didn't you let us know?" Lorrie called on her way up the walk. "If we hadn't stopped at Ben's for milk ..." her voice died as Rick brushed past her, jumped onto the porch, and drew Carol into a tight embrace.

"Don't!" Carol forced her hands between them, pushing against him. He had come at her too fast, his grip throwing her into a panic.

Rick dropped his arms and stepped away, confusion in his flint-colored eyes.

Lorrie stepped between them. "Rick hasn't changed a whit, still a bull in a china shop." Over her shoulder she said, "Ben warned us about her accident, Rick. How did you think she'd react to one of your rib-crunching hugs?"

"God, I'm sorry, Carol," Rick said. "I didn't think. I'm just so damn glad to see you again."

No reaction to my face. Ben must have warned them. Carol managed a smile. Rick had weathered over the years, she saw, grown a few inches taller, too. His tan was the kind that came from long days outdoors and the vertical crease between his eyes spoke of long hours squinting into the sun. Whip thin as he had been at sixteen, his face still all angles and planes, his cheekbones sharp enough to slice bread.

"It is so good to see you again, Caro. I can't tell you how much." Lorrie's gaze on her was steady. "Not so bad. Those scars will fade in no time."

Caro. No one but Lorrie had ever called her that.

A year older than Carol's thirty-eight, Lorrie's looks were the kind models spent hours achieving. She wore no makeup on her porcelain skin, only a copper-toned lipstick that matched her wild mane. She remained hipless as any boy, with legs that seemed to travel all the way to her neck, but her eyes remained her most arresting feature, irises an unusual yellow-gold rimmed in black. Cat eyes, Carol used to tease.

She almost brought that up, but reined the impulse in. They weren't kids any more. They weren't friends, either. Too many years apart, too many hurtful memories.

"How about coffee, you two? I just made fresh."

"Coffee sounds great," Rick answered, "but we can't stay long. We had dinner in Pendleton and brought pizza back for the boys. We stopped at Ben's for milk." He shook his head. "The boys go through a gallon a day."

Carol's eyes dropped to the wide gold band on Lorrie's hand. "When?"

Lorrie grinned. "After college. Rick insisted we wait for our degrees."

"I wanted to be sure she could support me in style," Rick joked.

"And you have sons," she said, herding them through the door. "How many, what are their names, how old are they?" A twinge of jealousy in her midsection. Childhood sweethearts happily married. Children. The kind of life she'd never have.

Lorrie laughed. "One teen, one about to be. The oldest is Richard Michael after you-know-who, and the youngest is Robert Graham, after my dad."

Carol motioned them to the kitchen table, filled three mugs with coffee, and placed chocolate chip cookies on a flowered plate.

Rick helped himself to two the minute the plate hit the table.

Lorrie stopped spooning sugar into her coffee. "You've got to be kidding. After the meal you just ate?"

A wolfish grin broadened his thin face. "I'm still a growing boy." He reached for another and bit into it with relish.

Lorrie shook her head in mock dismay, stirred her coffee, and took a cautious sip.

Carol steeled herself for the coming inquisition. Even as children, Rick and Lorrie had been direct, both in their questions and their opinions. She had admired that about them, tending toward shyness herself, but was in no mood for it now.

Lorrie set her coffee down and pinned Carol with her lioness eyes.

"So, stranger, what have you been up to all these years? Your Uncle James told us you worked at some college in Fairfield."

"Yes, in the English department."

"Doing what?"

"I'm the dean's assistant," Carol said, deciding a lie was better than the truth. "I lead a pretty boring life, actually. I go to work, I go home. I read and take walks. My idea of excitement is a stay at the coast on long weekends." Behind the lie Carol mourned the loss of her home, her job, her old life, gone now for good.

"Will is back, too, you know."

Don't get defensive Carol. She's making polite conversation, not probing for a reaction. "Ben mentioned that when he introduced me to Luce. She came into the store as I was leaving. He told me about Will's wife, too. What a shame."

"Yeah." Rick's voice softened. "They only had six months."

"What about Rose?" Carol remembered Will's mother, a kind, quiet woman who rarely spoke above a whisper.

"She died two years ago. Cancer."

"She deserved better."

"She had some good years, Carol," Lorrie said. "She and Will took off to Portland the year after you left. Rose became a library assistant. She loved her job."

"And Ray?" Carol hated asking, dreaded hearing he might still be around but wanting to be forewarned if he was.

"Bastard got drunk, passed out, and drowned in his own vomit," Rick said. "Couldn't have happened to a nicer guy."

Carol nodded. "I agree. The way he treated Will and Rose..." She changed the subject. "What about you two? What are you up to besides raising sons?"

Rick leaned back and hooked one arm over his chair. "I got my engineering degree at OSU." He freed his arm, pushed back from the table, and brought a foot up to rest on a knee. "I'm a hands-on sort of guy, so I spend a lot of time in the field."

Rick hadn't changed. Still full of nervous energy. No wonder he chose to work outdoors. Sitting behind a desk all day would drive him crazy.

"We raise a few cows, too." He nodded at Lorrie. "Your turn, honey."

"I taught kindergarten until the boys came," she said. "Now I substitute teach. I don't miss working full time. Between three men and fifty cows," a smile flickered across her mouth, "I keep busy enough."

"So you built a house here in the canyon?"

Rick shook his head. "No. We moved into my parents place. You remember it, the big log house a few miles from here?"

"I do. I loved that place. Do your parents live with you?"

"No. Dad passed away a couple of years ago. We bought the place from Mom. She moved to Arizona to live with her sister."

"Sorry about your dad, Rick. I didn't know."

"Thanks." Rick picked up his coffee and swallowed the last of it. "So, is your stay temporary or permanent?"

Carol hesitated, seeking a generic answer. "Right now I'm taking things easy, waiting for" – she gestured toward her face – "this to heal, but I must admit the temptation to stay is strong."

"Good. We'll keep our fingers crossed. Your Uncle James always hoped you'd come back here to live."

As though he'd said too much, Rick rose to his feet. "Don't mean to drink and run but we have to get on, our boys are probably chewing their fingers off by now."

"The only man I know who can drink his coffee while it's still boiling," Lorrie complained, taking a last, hurried sip of hers. She reached for her purse, and rifled through it for pen and paper.

"What's your phone number, Carol? I'll call you tomorrow and we can set a date for dinner at our place."

Carol reeled it off.

"Oh," Lorrie said. "You're keeping James' number?"

Carol shrugged. "I saw no reason to change it."

She walked them to their car. Before Rick got in, he gave her shoulder a gentle squeeze.

"Ouch. You're skin and bone, woman. We'll have to fatten you up."

Carol stood at the gate long after their car disappeared into the trees. The whistle from a coming train echoed across the creek, a melancholy sound in the gathering dusk. A few early stars winked in the deepening sky. For the first time since her return, the sight brought little solace.

\*\*\*

"Well," Lorrie said, once they reached the highway. "That felt awkward."

"It's been a long time, honey," Rick said. "You can't squeeze twenty plus years into a brief visit."

"I know." Lorrie scooted across the seat so that she could lean against his side. "But she seemed, I don't know, unhappy or embarrassed that we stopped by."

Rick patted her leg. "Caught off guard, that's all. We took her by surprise."

"Look out!"

Rick braked. "Don't worry, Hon, I see them." Two deer stood in the middle of the road, frozen by Rick's headlights. He flicked the lights off. When he turned them on again the deer were gone.

Lorrie smiled at her husband's profile

"You're staring, woman."

She sighed. "I know; bad habit of mine."

"Rick?"

"Yeah?"

"I almost asked why she didn't write."

"I'm glad you didn't. She's dealing with enough right now. Besides, you have to remember how overwhelmed she must have been back then – her parents' divorce, her mom taking her so far away. Heck of a lot for a fifteen-year-old kid to deal with."

"I guess you're right."

"What do you mean, you guess?" He patted her leg. "I'm always right."

Lorrie saw their porch light shining through the trees and her mood brightened. She loved coming home. In moments dogs and cats would surround them; their sons would stand in the doorway, clutching their stomachs, pretending starvation. Once inside the house they would be a world unto themselves.

She was one fortunate woman.

\*\*\*

After dinner Carol settled on the couch with a glass of wine and a book of Raymond Carver's poetry. She soon tossed the book aside. Not even Carver's vivid prose could push away the memories evoked by Rick and Lorrie's visit.

As children, the four of them, Rick, Lorrie, Will and her, had swam, hiked meadows and explored the canyon. On rainy days they played Scrabble or Monopoly. Summers were idyllic, each more perfect than the last, until her fifteenth year, the summer she fell in love with Will. But her happiness was marred by her parents' impending divorce and then, Will's stepfather found them together at the creek.

Carol pushed the painful images away, scrambled to her feet, and chose a CD of Beethoven Sonatas for the player.

On her way back to the sofa, she saw a figure at the window and froze. For what seemed an eternity she faced the intruder, until she realized the broomstick figure with ragged tufts of hair was herself, reflected in the glass.

Carol switched off the lamp before she sat down. She needed no reminder of what she'd become.

# 8

The man sits on a plastic-sheeted mattress and studies the earring on his palm.

Was she his third? Or maybe his fourth?

He glances toward the rounded top of an antique steamer trunk at the end of the bed, considers, and after a long moment, decides against opening it. His eyes return to the lusterless gem in his hand. Its wearer had been as false as the imitation stone, a seeker of pleasure from a total stranger. He'd given her pleasure and more. Thinking of that gives him a major hard-on.

Bernson, Cox, Jesperson. He'd studied them, fools all, letting blood lust override good sense. Trolling, Bundy called it. Well, he had that one right, at least. Cast the line, tease the water, wait for the strike, and set the hook. Of course, that egomaniac bragged he raised the bar by choosing victims from the visible world, rather than prostitutes and homeless women who moved unseen through mainstream society. Bundy might sneer at my style, but where's Bundy now?

I'm smarter. More focused. More controlled. In a word: superior. How many of my women have been found, three, four?

He unclenches his fist, holds the earring between thumb and forefinger, and raises it to catch the light from the bedside lamp. A shame the shine had worn off, but that doesn't keep him from reliving every exquisite moment he shared with its wearer. Her pain, so like the others, yet so unique; the crimson brightness of terror, the subtle nuances of gagged cries, the acrid tang of spilled urine, and above all, the sweet taste of bruising flesh. He groans and falls back on the bed, his hand reaching down.

Much later, when he locks the door to the room behind him, he whistles an aria from La Bohéme. That Puccini. What a romantic!

# 9

Carol's stomach turned over when Rick pulled into his driveway. Neither he nor Lorrie had mentioned other dinner guests when they invited her, yet several cars were parked along the fence.

Rick stopped in front of the barn, cut the engine, and twisted to face her.

"Lorrie was afraid you'd turn her down if she told you." His sun-browned hand reached to cover hers. "You've met Ben and Luce. Jackson Henry is here, and of course, Will."

Oh, God. Will too? She knew eventually she'd have to meet him, but this soon? And with this face? "Since my..." Carol paused, swallowed, "accident, people..." She started over. "I know they can't help reacting but that doesn't make it any less difficult."

"Human nature," Rick said. "People adjust. Before you know it, no one notices. Besides, what if the shoe were on the other foot?"

"It isn't." She knew how selfish that sounded but didn't care.

Rick squeezed her hand. "Okay, here's the deal. I can take you back home if you want. All I can say is that there are people in this world with more serious problems than a few measly scars."

Measly. She turned the word over in her mind. If you knew how I really got them. But his words stung. Carol withdrew her hand from his and reached for the door handle.

On their way up the walk Rick threw his arm around her shoulders.

This time, she didn't flinch.

\*\*\*

They entered a brightly lit kitchen filled with the mouthwatering scents of basil and roasting pork. Savory gravy simmered on the stove, and an island held cooling pies, purple juice bleeding through slits in the crust.

"We're here," Rick announced.

Lorrie stood at the stove, stirring a steaming kettle. Her face lit up with a smile. Her golden eyes held a plea for Carol alone: Don't be angry. Will stood next to Lorrie, his hands encased in oven gloves. All the air rushed from her lungs.

He looked the same and yet different. The bump on his nose – broken twice before he turned sixteen – and the squiggle of scar tissue bisecting one eyebrow were familiar. So was his dark hair, though it no longer brushed his collar. But loss had marked him. Sadness lived in the bottomless dark eyes now regarding her. Old hurt welled inside her even as a bubble of mirth lodged in her chest. Here stood the adult version of the boy she once desperately loved, wearing oven mitts for god's sake. This never happened in the movies. Where was the drama, the long lingering look, the tortured violin music playing in the background; better yet, a dark Rachmaninov concerto?

"Hi, Carol," he said.

"Will," she managed.

Lorrie broke the ensuing silence before it became awkward. "Better grab these potatoes and drain them, Will, or we'll be having mushed potatoes instead of mashed."

Will grinned. "Lorrie is the original kitchen Nazi. Excuse me, Carol, while I obey."

She nodded, not trusting her voice.

"Don't just stand there Rick," Lorrie said. "Pour Carol a glass of wine."

"Ja, Herr Obermeister." Rick clicked his heels with military precision and saluted before he reached for the open bottle on the counter.

Lorrie came around the stove and snapped her dishtowel at him. "Obermeister my, you-know-what," she said. A young boy raced into the kitchen. Lorrie squealed and jumped out of the way.

"You are so dead!" yelled an older boy on the heels of the younger one.

"Whoa," Rick yelled, "freeze, you two."

Rick introduced the oldest boy first. "Carol this is our fifteen-year-old, Richard Michael who usually has better manners. Mike, this is an old friend of ours, Carol Ingram."

The boy stepped forward and offered his hand. "Pleased to meet you, Miss Ingram. Please call me Mike. Everyone does."

Mike might have been cloned from his father. He had the same sharply chiseled features and flint-colored eyes, the same sandy hair, also the same quirky sense of humor, judging by his black sweatshirt. *Dear Algebra*, read bright red letters, *stop asking us to find your x. She's not coming back.*

"How do you do, Mike, I like your shirt." When he grinned he resembled Rick even more.

Her gaze went to the younger boy. "You must be Robert."

"Hi. You can call me Robbie."

If Mike took after Rick, Robert belonged to Lorrie. He had her copper hair and delicate features, the same devilish look in his eyes. Like his big brother he wore Levi's and a sweatshirt but a more sedate one, gray in color, with OSU in big orange letters and underneath, a vicious looking beaver.

"An Oregon State fan," she said. "Like your mom and dad."

He nodded, without taking his eyes from her face, though he seemed more fascinated than appalled by what he saw.

"Does that hurt?"

"Robert Donfield!" Lorrie snapped, whirling from the counter where she'd started whipping potatoes.

Robbie jumped, startled by his mother's tone.

"Only when I laugh," Carol answered, straight-faced.

"As you can see," Rick said, "Robert inherited his mother's tendency toward embarrassing bluntness."

Carol cocked an eyebrow. "His mother's?"

Lorrie groaned. "These two hellions will not be joining us for dinner. They're going to Pendleton with friends for hamburgers and a movie. Speaking of which, you two better get upstairs and change your clothes."

"Nice meeting you, Miss Ingram," they chorused before they hurried away.

"They're beautiful, Lorrie."

"We think so," Lorrie said, beaming. She gave the potatoes a few more vigorous stirs and set them in the warming oven.

"Okay," she said, removing her apron. "Time we joined the others. Will, I think it's safe to remove those mitts now. Rick, sweetheart, bring the wine.

# 10

A fire crackled in the massive native stone fireplace built by Rick's father. Candles glowed along the mantle.

Two men rose to their feet when they entered the living room, one more than a foot taller than the other.

"Caro," Lorrie said, "you've already met Ben. The man beside him is Jackson Henry."

"Hello again, Ben," Carol said. "How do you do, Jackson? I met your peacocks my first morning here."

A smile tugged the corners of his lips. "They do like to roam. I hope they haven't been a bother."

Unless you count scaring me half to death. "Not at all. They made quite a sight."

"Move those big buns, Jackson, so I can say hello."

Jackson flushed to the roots of his hair and stepped aside to reveal Luce curled in an oversized chair, dream catcher earrings glinting through her blonde hair.

"Hello, Luce, it's good to see you again."

When everyone was seated, Ben turned to her. "Solitude must agree with you, Carol. I've only seen you twice since you arrived."

"It does," Carol said.

"Lorrie tells me you two did a little breaking and entering when you were kids."

She laughed, suddenly at ease. You can do this, Carol. You used to be good at small talk. "I thought about that when I came to the store. You sure changed the place, Ben. When did you buy it?"

"Five years ago. I came to fish, noticed the For Sale sign, and when I saw the old oak cooler and brass cash register inside, I was hooked. That living quarters were included decided me. I took an early buy out from the Forest Service and bought and refurbished the place. Now I go fishing whenever I want."

"That's no joke," Rick said. "Wait until you need a quart of milk and find the *Gone Fishing* sign on the door."

"No one comes between Ben and his fly rod," Will said, with a good-natured jab to Ben's upper arm.

"Ouch!" Ben rubbed the spot, feigning pain. "Like you don't run me a close second."

Lorrie rose. "I think we can move to the table now, before Ben regales us with one of his fish stories."

Ben drew his eyebrows together, puckered his mouth in fake dismay, and grabbed the left side of his chest, miming pain. "Why Lorrie, you've cut me to the quick."

"You'll recover."

"Sharper than a serpents tooth," Ben said, which brought a laugh from everyone. He held his hand out to Carol. "Allow me to lead you to the dining room."

\*\*\*

After dinner they returned to the living room. Between the mesmerizing flames in the big stone fireplace and her full stomach, Carol was afraid to blink, fearful she'd fall asleep. She was glad when Rick and Lorrie arrived with fresh coffee and huckleberry pie a la mode.

Jackson, after one bite, broke into a beatific smile. "Man, this is good."

"Thank you, Jackson. We picked the berries last August. By the way, I've been meaning to ask how the new project is going."

"Really good," Jackson said. "I'm using Big Leaf Maple, Oregon grown, and aged since 1962." His face glowed. "Incredible grain."

Will spoke to Carol. "Jackson builds custom instruments for musicians."

"Do you get many orders, Jackson?" Luce asked. "I'd think living in the boondocks would make it difficult to get your name out there."

He shook his head. "Word of mouth brings me more orders than I can handle. Right now, my customer wait list is six years."

Ben whistled. "Whew! I had no idea."

"How about you, Will," Jackson said. "Landscaping business picking up?"

"It is. Unfortunately, I'm coming up short-handed, unless," he said with a smile, "you count my dog and Lady isn't into mowing and weeding. A couple of my crew decided to spend spring and summer hiking in the Cascades." He reached for his coffee. "I don't blame them. I'd go too if I could."

"Maybe Carol could fill one of those vacancies, Will," Luce said, giving him a sly glance.

"Hey, that's not a bad idea," Lorrie chimed in. "Sunshine and exercise. No one looking over your shoulder while you work – except for Will, of course." Her yellow eyes glowed. "What do you think, Caro?"

Caught off guard, Carol's face grew hot. Before she think of an answer, Will spoke.

"I am going to need extra hands, Carol. The work is physical but not too demanding. You might think about it."

"Thanks," she said. "I will. Think about it, I mean." Damn you Luce and Lorrie. Next time, mind your own business. Searching for a safer topic, she said, "I don't remember the logs being exposed when I was here before, Rick."

He cleared his throat and threw a knowing look at Lorrie.

"Don't you dare," she said.

He rubbed his hands together. "Exposing the logs was Lorrie's idea." He said. "She took a sledgehammer to the sheetrock that covered them."

"Wow, Lorrie," Luce said, impressed.

"Wow, indeed," Rick repeated, his tone wry.

"You'll pay for this, Rick Donfield."

Rick laughed. "My wife didn't realize the sheetrock was our only insulation then, or that we weren't the only ones who called this place home."

"I don't get it." Luce scooted to the edge of her chair, intrigued.

"In a word, bats," Rick intoned.

"Yuck." Luce hugged herself.

"I like bats, really I do," Lorrie broke in. "But not in the house."

"We spent all that night capturing bats and setting them free." Rick adopted a mournful tone. "Poor homeless things."

"You are such a drama queen," Lorrie said, slapping his thigh. "They went straight to the barn where they live happily to this day."

"If you say so, honey." Rick took a last bite of pie, scraping his fork across the plate to capture the last of the crumbs.

"Why not lick the thing and be done with it?" Lorrie chided.

"Can't help it, babe. Nothing tops your huckleberry pie." He stood up. "We need more coffee." He left the room, and returned with the pot.

A comfortable silence fell after he topped off cups.

Ben cleared his throat. His next words brought everyone up short. "I see by today's paper another body turned up. Near Crooked River, wasn't it Will?"

"I haven't seen today's paper."

Lorrie grimaced. "Wonderful after-dinner topic, Ben."

Carol had seen the article, but read no further than its headline. After Malone she had no stomach for that kind of news.

"She had children," Jackson said.

Ben rubbed his jaw. "So did the two other women they found last year, one near the McKenzie River in Eugene, the other near a river in Bend."

"Serial killer, you think?" Rick asked.

"Well," Ben said, "the news media isn't saying that but think about it. The women are single mothers. They were last seen in fairly popular watering holes, and their bodies were found in isolated locations near rivers." He shot a look at Will and Rick. "We've all fished Crooked River and the McKenzie and Deschutes. Lots of wild country to hide a body in."

Will nodded. "Hate to agree, but you're right. A lot of pickups and SUV's drive in close to fish. Be easy to dispose of a body without anyone noticing."

Ben turned to Jackson. "Didn't you come from Eugene – or was it Bend?"

Jackson leaned forward, hands grasping his knees. "I was raised in Eugene but I learned my craft in Bend."

Carol realized Jackson rarely looked directly at anyone for long. Rather, his gaze drifted over a shoulder, up to the ceiling, or like now, down at his knees.

Ben waited a beat. "So, how did you end up here?"

Jackson raised his head. "My mentor and his wife came one summer to visit friends and he fell in love with the country." He leaned back, crossing his hands over his stomach. "After he died, I came to see the place for myself. I fell in love, too."

"But you go back to Bend every year, don't you?" Lorrie asked. "For workshops, I think you said."

Carol watched, fascinated, as the big man glanced at the ceiling, then at his hands before making eye contact with Lorrie. "Yes, twice a year. I visit high school wood shops and I teach a master class at colleges in Bend and Eugene."

"You're a busy guy," Luce said.

A blush crept up his face.

Ben saved him from further embarrassment. "By the way, having mentioned rivers, anyone care to join me in Sunriver this year? We could have quite a time together."

"Oh, no you don't, Ben Wagner." Lorrie jumped up. "Before we call it a night we need to schedule our spring party. You can talk about fishing then." She walked to a desk beneath a window, opened a drawer, and pulled out a small calendar. "Two weeks from now. Is that enough notice, do you think?"

Ben shrugged. "Any time works for me."

Jackson nodded assent.

"It's tradition, Carol, Luce," Lorrie said. "Every year, spring and fall, we have a party. Everyone brings a favorite recipe. We provide liquid refreshment and decorations. We set up a dance floor, too, in the pasture next to the barn."

"I love a party," Luce said.

"Carol?" Lorrie said.

"Sure. Count me in."

"Good," Lorrie said. "I'll probably ask your help with decorations."

With that, the evening wound down. Everyone got up and against Lorrie's wishes, carried their plates and cups to the kitchen.

"Don't worry, Ben," Luce said, brushing against him. "I won't drop anything."

His mouth twitched. "I sure hope not," he said, but his voice held laughter.

"Can I drive you home? It's on my way," Ben said, as he and Carol entered the kitchen. "It will save Rick time since Lorrie has him on dish duty tonight."

Rick groaned. "A curse on your house, Ben Wagner, taking pleasure in my pain. I'll even the score one day."

Ben slapped him on the back. "To borrow a phrase the younger generation remains fond of: You wish."

***

Ben started the car and slipped a CD in the player. "Hope you like Ella."

"I do, very much." Carol settled back, content. She had enjoyed the evening and glad Rick's little lecture convinced her to stay. No one but little Robert showed interest in her appearance, and he had been fascinated, not horrified. Of course, Lorrie and Rick may have forewarned Will and Jackson. Still...

After a few moments, Ben lowered the volume. "You had a good time tonight, I trust."

"I did. Rick and Lorrie are wonderful hosts." Carol glanced at him. "Company wasn't bad, either."

He chuckled. "I understand the four of you go back quite a way."

"We do." In her mind's eye Carol saw the three of them on the day she first met them. Lorrie, with her striking yellow eyes and copper hair; Rick, all elbows and knees and flashing teeth; Will, dark eyes shuttered, a fading bruise on one side of his face. "My uncle introduced us my first summer here."

Ben cleared his throat. "I hear Will's stepfather was one mean son of a bitch. Rick's words, not mine."

"Rick's right. Ray treated Will and his mom badly."

"I hear he got what he deserved in the end."

Did Ben expect a response? She wouldn't give him one. She didn't want to think about Ray Zabransky after such a pleasant evening.

"I think I've brought up an unpleasant subject," Ben said. "I apologize."

"No need. I guess I was remembering what Will went through, and his mother. That's the unpleasant part."

After that, neither spoke until Ben pulled up to her gate.

"Thanks, Ben."

"My pleasure. I'll see you to the door." He set the parking brake and undid his seat belt. "A gentleman always sees a lady to the door."

\*\*\*

After Ben left, Carol checked the deadbolt, then checked locks on the downstairs windows. "Always check twice," her mom used to preach, and Carol did, though she knew how useless locks were when you trusted your keys to the wrong person.

She put a Segovia CD on the player and curled on the sofa, enjoying the music, not yet sleepy enough for bed. Much as she had enjoyed her evening, she was glad to be home.

Home. She tasted the word. Until now, she hadn't allowed herself to use it. She dropped her head back against the sofa and closed her eyes.

A moment later, the phone rang, shattering the quiet.

Probably Lorrie, calling to say good-night. But when Carol answered, a definite click followed her greeting.

Wrong number? Caller too embarrassed to apologize because of the late hour? A logical explanation, so why the squiggle of fear through her midsection? Everyone dialed a wrong number at one time or another, including her. No reason for paranoia.

But her unease lingered, even after she turned out the light and headed upstairs to bed.

# 11

In the morning Luce left for the store to get a dozen eggs and Will went outside to work in his garden. Discovering a clump of Forget-Me-Nots brought him up short. They had been Jordan's favorite flower.

After eight years, grief no longer tormented him, but seeing the delicate periwinkle-blue flowers turned back the clock.

Jordan. She had kissed him awake that last morning; that last, incredibly normal-seeming morning.

"Lady and I are going for a run, sweetheart. Be back in a few."

His gaze ran over her running shorts, the oversized U of O shirt that almost covered them, her shining face, devoid of makeup, and pulled her into his arms.

"Plenty of exercise to be had here at home, Ms. Jacobs," he whispered into her hair. "I can offer you a great, aerobic workout without your ever leaving this room."

She disentangled herself, laughing.

"We'll return bearing gifts," she promised, "Cranberry-orange scones and Starbuck's strongest."

She blew him a kiss from the door. Defeated, Will reached for his book on the bedside table, and settled back against the pillows. A long, lazy weekend lay ahead. He was in no mood to hurry it.

As he would later learn, a silver Lexus raced through a red light and hit both Jordan and Lady. The impact catapulted both out of the crosswalk. Jordan died instantly. Lady barely survived and took weeks to mend.

For six months, he lived on auto-pilot. He went to work. He visited Lady at the vet's while she recuperated, came home afterward and stared at the walls. He fingered Jordan's clothes and slept with her robe. When Lady came home she roamed from room to room, whining, carrying one of Jordan's slippers in her mouth. His mother offered no platitudes, but her presence, along with Lady's, kept him from going entirely mad.

Then, one morning, he woke clear-headed. He packed Jordan's things and took them to a thrift store. He moved out of their neighborhood and into a new one, taking nothing of their life together but his three favorite photographs of her.

*Field Notes.* I was reading *Field Notes* when Jordan died.

# 12

"Hmmm. Daughter of King Minos." Ben counted the blocks on the crossword, nodded, and printed Ariadne in number thirty-nine across.

Done.

He folded the newspaper, noticing the article about the woman found at Crooked River. He shouldn't have brought that up last night. Lorrie was right to chastise him. He hadn't thought how it might affect Carol, living alone. But that business happened clear across the state, far from Winter.

He liked Carol. A woman not compelled to fill every minute with meaningless chatter. Shame about her accident, though he found it strange she could go through a windshield and only sustain damage to one side of her face. None of his business, of course.

He pushed away from the table, got to his feet and walked outside to put the newspaper in the recycling bin. Before he raised the lid, he stopped to admire the view. The meadow and hills across the road grew greener each day. A flash of movement registered in his peripheral vision. He turned his head and saw Cora moving outside her bungalow, a few hundred yards away.

Ben felt a rush of gratitude for this place he called home

He was about to go inside when the Honda sped into the parking lot and braked, sending gravel flying.

Luce. He knew without looking. Will never drove like that.

# 13

Carol applied fresh lipstick and ran her fingers through hair that refused to lay flat. She took her list from the kitchen table, pulled her keys from her purse and headed for the car. Grocery day. She wanted to buy a few houseplants, too, and an art print to hang on the wall.

She'd gone ten miles when a muffled thump came from outside the car and the steering wheel jerked to the right. She pulled onto the shoulder and stopped. Please God, not a flat tire. She turned off the engine, set the emergency brake, and got out. One look and she knew her prayer went unheard. Well, at least it wasn't pouring rain.

She popped the trunk and rummaged in the well for the lug wrench and jack.

Of course, once she got the sprocket on the lug nut, no amount of straining could budge the darn thing – or any of the others, she soon learned. She stepped on the cross piece and bounced up and down. The lug seemed to give a fraction.

Renewing her efforts, she didn't notice the brown Chevy pickup until it pulled in ahead of her car.

Relax, she told herself. This isn't the city. People here stop to help, not to mug. All the same, her stomach tightened.

"Hello again."

Oh God. Where's a mugger when you need one?

"Hi, Will." She stepped off the tire iron with as much grace as possible.

"Here, let me." Will bent to the tire iron but she stopped his hand.

"I've done this before, Will. I'm fine, really. Thanks anyway."

"At least let me loosen the rest of the lug nuts, Carol. Even I have a problem with the damn things."

She squared her shoulders – firmly, she hoped. "Honest, Will. I can handle it. Ignoring him, she squatted down and redoubled her efforts.

Unsuccessfully.

"Suit yourself." Will's tone was carefully neutral. "Maybe I'll see you later."

His words proved prophetic. Much later, he passed her going back toward town. She had just finished tightening the last lug on her spare and was hauling the jack and iron to the trunk.

He beeped.

From the brief glimpse she caught of him, she was pretty sure he was laughing.

After a moment, she did too. Why on earth had she thought it so important that Will think her capable of changing a stupid tire?

Hours later, Carol left Pendleton with four new tires and everything on her list. Just past Mission, an old Cadillac pulled from a side road into her path. Carol wound up following it all the way back to Winter at twenty-five miles an hour, even in the fifty-five mile zone. The invisible driver — Carol couldn't see a head above the driver's seat — rode the center line, making it impossible to pass. By the time she crossed Sorrow Creek, still behind the ancient car, her stomach was growling like a cat in heat.

\*\*\*

Home at last, Carol slapped a peanut butter and jelly sandwich together and took it with a tall glass of milk onto the deck to eat in the sun. After she finished, she went back inside and set about choosing homes for her new houseplants. The two-colored ivy went on top of the fridge, the birds-nest fern on the coffee table and both African violets she placed on the window ledge in the downstairs bathroom where they'd receive plenty of indirect light. She leaned the Matisse print she'd purchased against the living room wall where she hoped to hang it. She'd need to ask Lorrie for help with that.

Now for a walk.

She headed for the bridge, crossed it, and followed a deer trail upstream through stands of alder and jack pine. Quail chattered in willows near the water. Sparrows darted from branch to branch, appearing and disappearing with lightning speed. Twenty minutes brought her out of the trees to a wide bend in the creek where a tall boulder jutted from the water. Hoisting herself up, she wrapped her arms around her knees and closed her eyes, enjoying the sun on her face and the rush of moving water. She, Rick, Lorrie and Will used to swim here. They'd paddle across the creek, climb the bluff on the opposite side and jump, laughing, from its highest point. On some days they brought food, and after swimming, built small campfires on the rocks to roast hotdogs and marshmallows. They drank lemonade sealed in Mason jars they weighted in the shallows to stay cool.

Lost in the past, Carol didn't hear him approach. When a hand fell on her shoulder, she screamed, and would have tumbled from her perch but for the arms that caught and pinned her. Unable to see her attacker, she struggled, tried kicking back, hoping her foot might connect with a shin. She tried biting the arms that held her but couldn't stretch far enough to reach one. At last, a voice made its way through her blind struggle.

"Carol! It's me. Will. I called but I guess the creek drowned out my voice. I'm sorry; I didn't mean to frighten you."

She stopped struggling. For the second time that day she'd made a fool of herself in front of him. Was this some cosmic joke?

She turned to face him, feeling her face burn. "Hi again. You must think I'm nuts, reacting the way I did."

"No. We don't. Coming up on you like that? I would have jumped, too."

We? Carol looked down. A big Doberman stood at Will's side, one liquid brown eye trained on her. The other was sewn shut.

"This is Lady." Will laid his hand on the dog's head.

Old scars crisscrossed the dog's black hide; only a stub remained of one ear flap.

The sight made her queasy. "What happened to her?"

"She was hit by a car. It happened a long time ago."

Dropping to her knees, she held her hand under Lady's nose. After a brief sniff, a long pink tongue came out and lapped her palm.

"As you can see, she's a pussy cat." Will fingered the leather strap on his binoculars. "This is a great spot. I come here to keep an eye on the eagles."

"Where?"

He pointed to three pines on top of the ridge. "There. I was lucky enough to see the female building her nest. Did you know she can carry sticks three times her size?"

"No, I didn't." Carol narrowed her eyes, tried to follow the direction his finger pointed, but couldn't make out the nest. "I'll leave you and Lady to it then."

"No reason we can't both share the spot."

A breeze came off the water, ruffling her hair. She tried smoothing it down without success.

"The punk rocker look suits you." Will voice was gentle.

"That's me, ever the trend setter," she quipped, suddenly awkward.

"Carol."

She steeled herself. Please, Will, no facile remarks about the past.

"I think you should know I was on the hill above your house," he held out the binoculars, "with these, the day you arrived."

Huh?

"It's another good place for viewing the nest. I thought you were a trespasser at first. I left when I realized."

So he knew I was here before anyone told him.

"I see." She dropped her eyes to Lady, now pressed against her leg. "Well, thanks for allowing me my privacy that day. I was dead on my feet after the long drive."

She stepped back, shading her eyes with her hand. "I really have to get home. Say hi to Lucinda for me, won't you?"

"I'll do that. Oh, wait." He reached into his vest pocket. "I found something that might interest you." His hand came out with a smooth, rock the size of a hen's egg, speckled with brown and white, and veined with silver. "Still collecting?"

"I gave it up after we left Winter."

"Maybe you can start again."

She took the rock, warm from his hand. "Maybe. Thank you, Will, it's beautiful"

His eyes held hers a fraction too long before she turned away.

***

That evening after dinner, Carol slipped on a sweater, grabbed a flashlight, and headed for the creek. When she got there a few stars glittered in the dusky sky. Nighthawks and bats swooped and dived over the water, feasting on their evening meal. Soon, the moon crested the ridge, opening a silver path across the creek. Droplets of water sparkled on the rocks and moonlight tinseled the trees, turning them into a child's dream of Christmas. How had she had lived so long away from this? For a moment what happened in California no longer mattered. Not the loss of her home and job, not Malone's craziness. Maybe her mood wouldn't last, but for now she had the bright moon, the silvery creek, and the luminous trees. She had friends, a home, a chance for a new life, a better life than the one she left behind. She had a future.

# 14

Lorrie came the next afternoon to help Carol hang her print. "I'm glad you called," she said. "Now I won't mind roping you in to help me decorate Saturday."

Sun streamed through the open windows, bringing the scent of lilacs with it. A cat bird cried from the meadow, living up to its name. Lorrie took in the new throw pillows on the sofa, the fern nestled in its earthenware pot, and smiled approval. "Little changes, but they do make a difference. Oh, this is pretty," she said, picking up the rock Carol left on the coffee table. "Did you bring it with you from California?" Without waiting for an answer, she put the rock back and leaned down to examine the fern. "Hope you have better luck with these than I do. I love ferns, but after a week mine start to turn brown and before long, it's 'hasta la vista, baby'."

"So far it's holding its own," Carol said. "Here's a pencil. If you like my choice for the Matisse, mark the spot." She picked the print up and held it against the wall. "Here? And please hurry, this is heavy."

"No, a little to the right. Wait, too much. Move it back a couple of inches. There!" Lorrie hurried over and made a fine mark on the wall. "Now, you can set it down."

"Looks good, doesn't it?" Carol said, after she hammered in a hook and they maneuvered the print in place.

Lorrie snorted. "Personally, I think the artist had depth perception problems. Why does that bowl of fruit look like it's sliding off the table? Oh, yeah, because the table is tilting at an impossible angle. Maybe one of its legs is broken?"

Carol laughed. "Philistine!" She adjusted the print a fraction, stood back again, and nodded with satisfaction. "How about a glass of wine to mark this momentous event?"

Lorrie ran a hand ran through her wild hair, fell into a chair, and crossed her long legs. "You bet. Then you can tell me what you and Will talked about when you met at the creek."

Carol, on her way to the kitchen, turned. "What? How did you....? Oh. Of course. Will told Rick, and Rick –"

"Tells me everything," Lorrie finished smugly. Her voice followed Carol to the kitchen. "Don't try changing the subject because I'm not leaving until you tell all."

"All amounts to nothing," Carol said when she returned with a tray holding two glasses of wine, crackers and Brie.

"Umm, I love Brie." Lorrie helped herself to the cheese first, then picked up her wine. "Here's lookin' at you kid," she said, and brought the glass to her mouth.

Carol burst out laughing at Lorrie's reaction to her first taste of the wine.

"Wow," she said, her eyes wide. "This is no bargain basement hooch. Where on earth did you get it?"

"I thought you'd like it. Uncle James had a few bottles tucked away in the pantry."

"Sorta spoils me for the eight dollar bargains Rick brings home. I'll have to help you hang art more often." After a second, longer sip, Lorrie set her glass down. "Okay. You and Will. I'm all ears."

"There's nothing to tell. Will and I ran into each other by accident." Carol reached for a cracker. "He introduced me to Lady. What a sweet dog. He told me she'd been hit by a car years ago. From the look of her I'd say it's a miracle she survived."

"Is that all he said, she was hit by a car?"

"Yes, why?"

A slight frown pinched the bridge of Lorrie's nose. "Just wondered. So what else did you two talk about?"

"We didn't. The entire episode lasted less than ten minutes."

Lorrie set her glass down with care. "Let me get this straight," she said, her tone disbelieving, "you two haven't seen one another in years, you're alone at the creek, yet neither of you takes advantage of the chance to catch up?"

"What, I'm going to ask him about his life, knowing the man lost his wife and his mother? And why would Will have any interest in mine? He answered one letter after I wrote. I never heard from him again." Carol dropped her eyes to her hands. "Or you either, for that matter. I kept writing but not one of you answered."

"Whoa. I wrote. We all did. We had one letter from you but after that, nothing. We asked your Uncle James if anything was wrong and he said you were probably too busy getting settled and we'd hear from you later. We never did."

Carol wet her lips. The truth she'd avoided, one she hadn't wanted to believe, now impossible to ignore. "My mother," she whispered.

"Your mother?" Lorrie said. "What about her?"

"She destroyed the letters." That this hadn't occurred to her before stunned her. Or maybe it had, and she'd never found the nerve to confront it.

They'd barely settled in California when she started throwing up every morning. At first her mother had been sympathetic, reassuring. "Nerves, sweetheart," she'd insisted. "The move has been hard on both of us. But before long, her mother realized the truth: her fifteen-year-old daughter was pregnant. She didn't blame Carol. She blamed her brother, James, and the boy – she suspected Will – who took advantage of her. No wonder she decided to break off all contact with Winter. Carol started school that year six weeks pregnant. Three weeks later, under the horrified stares of her classmates, she miscarried during biology lab.

How much anguish might have been avoided had she told her uncle and mother the truth? She'd been too scared, her need to protect Will paramount, and later, she had been too bitter by what she considered his betrayal.

A strangled laugh escaped her. What a conversation they might have had when they met at the creek.

"So, Carol. Too busy to write?"

"Darn morning sickness made it impossible."

"What?"

"Oh, yes, seems I was pregnant when I left Winter."

Some conversation.

"Carol? Are you okay?"

Lorrie's voice, weighted with concern, forced her back to the moment. "I told Mom I hated her for making us move. She kept insisting we needed a fresh start, a new life for ourselves." A pulse throbbed in Carol's temple. She pressed two fingers against it. "I gave her my letters. She stopped at the post office every day to collect mail" A memory surfaced: her mother, refusing to look at her when she said there wasn't any mail. And I thought it was because she couldn't bear to see the hurt in my eyes. "I was such a brat, Lorrie. My father had left us, she had a new job and me to worry about, and all I did was complain." The throb in her temple increased. "I guess she decided I needed a dose of reality."

"I'm sorry," Lorrie said, her voice gentle. "It must have been a terrible time for both of you. I might not understand your mother's reasoning but I know one thing for sure. She loved you very much. That was always obvious." She got up and joined Carol, wrapping her in an embrace. "Now that we know what really happened, we can put it behind us. Welcome home, Caro."

# 15

Saturday promised clear skies and plenty of sun. Carol, dressed in sneakers, jeans, and a red tee, was in the kitchen boxing her contributions for the potluck: two salads, deviled eggs, and pot stickers with dipping sauces. Her party dress and shoes lay on the sofa with her makeup bag. After she finished decorating with Lorrie, she'd shower and change in the guestroom.

She glanced at the clock. Two-thirty. Carol couldn't help her, 'first-time-they-see-me' jitters. Attending the party meant meeting more people. She had to get used to that. Turning into a recluse because of her face would be letting Malone win.

When Lorrie's knock came she hurried to answer the door.

"Ready?" Lorrie stood on the threshold. "Sorry I'm so late. Tore a shoelace tying my sneakers and it took me forever to remember where I put my spares."

"Come on in. I need help carrying things to the car," Carol said. "Your hair looks nice. And that clip is gorgeous."

Lorrie had piled her lustrous hair on top of her head and fastened it in place with a beaded clip shaped like a butterfly.

"Thanks." Her hand touched the clip. "Grace Blue Hawk made this for me. She and Louis are coming today. You're going to love them. Wish their niece was coming, but she's gone home to Montana to visit her mother."

***

Minutes later they were on their way. While Lorrie drove, Carol gazed at the river, green as jade in the morning light. She saw two blue herons, each in his own spot, both so still they resembled garden statuary more than living, breathing creatures.

Lorrie slowed so she could point to a dirt road on her left. "Will's turnoff."

Carol nodded. "Yes, the road to Cora's old place. Rick pointed it out the night he brought me to dinner." She turned her attention back to the river. "You picked a perfect day for the party, Lorrie. It's gorgeous."

"I have to agree. If it stays this clear—hold on!"

Lorrie hit the brakes as a rusted Ford pickup flew into their path.

Carol was thrown forward first, then jerked back when her seat belt caught.

The driver of the pickup gunned the engine and sped away, oily black smoke trailing from his exhaust.

"Damn idiot. Are you okay, Carol?"

"I'm fine. Boy, those are some reflexes you have. Who was that? Better yet, what was that?"

Lorrie started forward, her eyes fixed on the road. "There's a camp about two miles down that road he blew out of. Weird bunch, claim to be survivalists but I think they're druggies – users, makers, pushers, or all three. I see the police helicopter circling the area but so far haven't heard of any arrests."

"So even Winter isn't safe from the drug trade."

"No, its isolation makes it perfect. And that's something you need to keep in mind when you're out walking. Before you arrived the State Police discovered a marijuana crop a few miles from your place. They didn't catch the growers but they did find a camp where the lookouts stayed. They got away but left everything behind, including two shotguns."

"Wow," Carol murmured.

"By the way," Lorrie said, changing the subject. "Will is helping Rick string lights. I told him about the mix up with the letters. I hope you don't mind."

"No, of course not." But Carol did mind. She'd rather Will go on believing she'd forgotten him than have him think less of her mother who, no matter how misguided, only meant to protect her daughter.

She leaned back against the seat and closed her eyes.

# 16

After he finishes breakfast, he cuts the article from the newspaper. He washes his hands before removing a roll of clear tape from the kitchen drawer. Carrying both to his room, he examines the walls, finds a space, and tapes the clipping there, between older versions of similar reports. His hands clench as he steps back and rereads the article.

> "Acting on an anonymous tip, police today arrested Marjory Gilman at her residence in northeast Portland. Ms. Gilman, who has a long record of drug abuse and prostitution, allegedly sold her three- and five-year-old daughters to pedophiles in exchange for drugs. Both children have been placed with Children's' Services Division pending further investigation. Anyone with information is asked to contact Detective Maureen Sellers at the Multnomah Branch of

the Portland Police Department. Names will be held in strictest confidence."

He shakes his hands to relieve their stiffness and moves to the bed. The mattress shifts as he lowers his weight onto it. Reverently, he removes a jewelry case from the bedside table. The black velvet cover is worn from handling. There are days he almost forgets, until a new atrocity appears in the headlines, and like a biblical Golem of old, the past rises up from the bitter dust of memory to seize and shake him with its fury.

\*\*\*

The movie's been over for hours. The ticket booth is dark, and they are alone on the deserted street except for a wild-eyed man with torn newspapers tucked inside his ragged coat. He's waving his arms at them, stomping his feet, and screaming, "Demons! Demons want my soul." Alec moans, his small body vibrating with terror. The last time the crazy man stumbled toward them, wetness spread across the front of Alec's ratty jeans. Mom will be mad, the boy thinks. She'll spank Alec again because she says five is too old to pee in your pants. The boy looks up and down the dark street. Where is she? She said she'd pick them up after the movie. She looked so pretty when she let them off, her yellow hair all curly, her best earrings sparkling; the sequins on her new blue dress shining like stars when they caught the light.

He had tried to touch them, but she had slapped his hand away. "Mom has a hot date, sweetie. Don't muss me."

He got the scary feeling then, because she was talking in her funny voice – high and hurried, like she can't catch her breath, like she sounded the night she put him on the roller coaster at the fair and forgot to come back for him.

A car! She's here. He grabs Alec's hand and moves toward the curb. The car speeds past.

Please, please, don't let her forget us again. The last time she was gone for three days. He'd been scared then, too, but at least he and Alec were home – not standing in the dark with a crazy man and having to pee with no place to go.

The pain in his stomach is back. Mom promised them hamburgers after the movie, with fries and chocolate shakes. He knows it's too late now.

"Hey!"

Mom! She didn't forget! The pain in his stomach disappears like magic. He puts his hand on Alec's shoulder and guides him toward the car, but when they get close, his stomach lurches, and the pain comes back, only worse this time.

There's a man in the car.

"Goddammit, hurry up you two," his mother hisses.

Swallowing hard, the boy herds Alec into the back seat. Well-attuned to his mother's moods, he touches Alec's lips with a gentle finger then places his arm around his little brother's narrow shoulders for the ride home. Alec, wet, tired and hungry, slumps against him, asleep before the car pulls away from the curb.

When they reach home, his mother and the stranger stagger, laughing, into the house, leaving him in the car with the sleeping Alec. He half-carries, half-drags Alec up the walk, through the front door and down the hall to their bedroom. He can hear his mother and the man in the kitchen; his mother's fevered laugh sounds like breaking glass.

Undressing Alec, the boy throws the damp and smelly jeans into the back of the closet. By the time mom finds them, he hopes they will be dry. A wave of fury shakes him. What's a little guy supposed to do when he's hungry and scared and has to pee and no one comes to get him? He strips down to his underwear and climbs under the covers. Tomorrow, Mom won't remember forgetting them, or not feeding them. She won't remember much of anything. The boy hopes the man is gone by then. Before he turns out the light, he glances at Alec. He's such a good little kid. He hardly ever cries. The boy thinks Alec learned early on that tears helped nothing.

He was the same age, five, when Mom brought Alec home. He remembers Alec's baby fingers closing tightly over his own, remembers the fierce love that gripped him at that moment.

For as long as he can remember, his mom has been two people. One of them sometimes stays in bed for hours – days, even, and doesn't recognize them when they try to wake her. When that happens, the boy makes breakfasts and packs lunches for two before going to school, otherwise, his little brother will go unfed until the boy returns in the afternoon.

The other mom, the happy one, makes pancakes for breakfast, with chocolate chips in them, and oatmeal cookies with M & M's instead of raisins, because Alec likes the pretty colors. When she's not sick, she reads to them at bedtime, and hugs them tight, and says, "Don't let the bedbugs bite." She even sings a lullaby the boy knows by heart, and during the bad times, when they have no pancakes, no cookies, no song, Alec begs, "Sing me, please, sing me," and the boy sings, "Hush little baby don't you cry, brother's gonna sing you a lullaby…"

The boy is drifting off to sleep when Alec wakes and whines. "I'm thirsty."

"Better not Alec, Mom has company. We can't leave the room when she has company."

"I be quiet," Alec promises, his voice small. "I get it in the bathroom. Mommy won't hear."

For the rest of his life he is haunted by the sound of Alec's small feet padding over the bedroom's bare floor, the sliver of light that sneaked into the room when he opened the door, and moments later, the shrill cry, so quickly cut off, the thud against a wall. The front door slammed before his mother's frantic screams brought the boy running. He finds her on the floor, Alec in her arms. Alec is limp, his eyes open, but unseeing. Blood pumps from his head, running down his face and over their mother. Her screams raise goose bumps on the boy's skin. He sees that one of her earrings has fallen from her ear and lies on the floor like a fallen star. He reaches for it, folds it tightly in his palm.

Sirens. Men in white, men in blue. The boy watches Alec being wheeled from the house on a stretcher. An ambulance waits at the curb, its spinning red light slicing the air into crimson shards, coloring the faces of neighbors drawn outside by the noise. Two policemen escort his mother, wrapped in a blanket, to a waiting patrol car. A stern-looking woman with liquid brown eyes explains that his brother and mother have to go away for a while but he's going to stay with a nice family until everything gets better.

He opens his mouth to ask when, finds he forgot how to talk.

"Wuh...wuh...when will ma...ma...mom and...ah... ah...Alec cuh...come?"

She hesitates, biting her lip. "I'm not sure," she finally answers.

He never sees Alec again.

***

Oblivious to the tears wetting his face, the man opens the jewelry case and fingers the contents, need rising inside him. He traces a tiny gold dragonfly with one finger, moves on to a sterling silver round with a pink stone in its center. A few are quite valuable, like the one with diamonds of dew glistening on gold rose petals. He removes that one, lets it rest on his palm. She was his fifth – no, his sixth. He replaces the earring, one of twenty, each separated from its twin, separated as he was from Alec. With a sigh, he closes the lid and returns the box to the drawer. His hands grip his thighs, digging into muscle. He glances at the trunk. The temptation is strong but he has no time to indulge. The day promises to be a busy one, many things to do. Later, he promises himself, later.

# 17

Luce stood on the Donfield's wide lawn, admiring the colored lights strung along the roofline and porch, the multicolored votives on top of fence posts. In the fading light the flames within flickered like fireflies captured in glass.

"Evening, Luce."

"Hey, Ben." A fleeting smile touched her lips. She swept her hand over the scene. "Beautiful, isn't it?"

"Sure is. Rick and Lorrie know how to throw a party."

His hand came to rest on the small of her back. "You're looking wistful. Something bothering you?"

She edged away. "I'm never wistful, Ben, you know that. I'm having a quiet moment."

"Right. You. A quiet moment. A woman who hates quiet. What's the problem?"

Luce bit her lip. Silly, after all this time, to care.

"A couple of the women think I want to steal their pudgy, boring, husbands." She tossed her head. "Can I help it if their men come sniffing around?"

Ben chuckled. "Do I hear a Tammy Wynette song in the background? Sure you're not overreacting? Your 'don't mess with me' attitude is rather daunting, you know."

"Don't patronize me, Ben. I know what daunting means. And I'm not overreacting. Given half a chance, those two would fall on me like wolves on a pregnant doe."

Luce ignored his exasperated sigh. Ben didn't know her as well as he thought; didn't know how she ended up alone at thirteen, scared and hungry; what she did to survive. Men with gold bands on their ring fingers had been the worst. She shivered.

Ben noticed. "Are you cold?"

Luce shook her head. "No. Goose walking over my grave, I guess."

"Well, perk up. Here comes Jackson."

Luce followed Ben's gaze and saw Jackson Henry walking toward them, paper cups in hand.

"Th..thought you two might be th...thirsty," he said.

"Thanks, big man," Luce said, taking one. "Very thoughtful of you." She lifted the cup to her mouth and drank. "Umm, good. I wonder what's in it."

"Lemonade, raspberry syrup, orange juice and club soda." Jackson grinned. "I helped Lorrie make it."

Beside him, Luce felt like Thumbelina from the fairy tale, an all-too-breakable Thumbelina. Her eyes drifted to his hands, skittered away.

"I hope you'll sss ... save me a waltz, Luce."

Jackson's hopeful look made her smile. "I'd be honored."

"Thank you. I'll come back for you. Right now, Rick needs me at the barbecue pit." He turned to Ben. "See you later, Ben."

Ben punched Jackson lightly on the arm. "Not to dance with, I hope."

Without missing a beat, Jackson replied. "Da...darn. I thought we'd make a great tango team."

"I get such a kick out of that sly humor of his," Ben said after Jackson left. "He's usually so reserved." He raised an eyebrow. "You notice Jackson only stutters around you, Luce? Guy has a crush. Should I be jealous?"

Baiting her. Well, she wasn't one of Ben's prize fish. She wasn't taking the pretty fly anymore. Damn it anyway. Why did she always fall for the wrong men?

*"Call Ben if you need anything," Will said, before leaving for Portland to close the sale on his condo, so that afternoon she took the river path to the store, arriving at Ben's back door out of breath and regretting her decision to walk. When he answered her knock his face broke into a wide smile. "Look who's here! Come in."*

*She entered a room that ran the width of the store, living room separated from kitchen by a waist high counter. She'd never spent much time in kitchens, but she recognized class when she saw it. The stainless steel appliances were top of the line, including the coffee maker that was the only object on the granite countertops.*

*It struck her that his place held no personal objects, no family pictures, or pictures of friends. The only thing that contrasted with the leather sofa and chair, the chrome and glass coffee table, was a scarred library table pushed against the staircase wall, with its scattering of feathers and a vise attached to one edge.*

*"I was tying flies," he said.*

*He served coffee in delicate china along with a dish of raw sugar cubes and cream in a jug that matched the china. Luce felt pampered and more than a little touched. He was also a great listener. She found herself telling him about Will's mother and how much she missed her. Under his sympathetic gaze, his mesmerizing blue eyes, she let slip her reason for coming to Winter. Too late, she realized she'd revealed too much. Other than Ben's mention of a brief early marriage and divorce, and his regret that his job had required frequent moves that left no time for relationships, she'd learned nothing about him.*

*"I live a monk's life," he'd kidded.*

*When she got up to leave, he offered to drive her. Had she made the first move, or did he orchestrate what happened? She still didn't know. All she remembered was his mouth covering hers, his hands moving over her body. Her heated response.*

"Bet I know what you're thinking." Ben's amused voice jerked her back to the present. He tapped her earring and set it swinging.

She batted his hand away. "Don't."

"You never take them off, do you? Maybe Will means more to you than you let on."

A young girl moved through Luce's peripheral vision, a girl in a flowered dress with pink and green ribbons streaming from her blonde hair. Was she real or the ghost of herself in happier times, before she lost her parents?

"What's going on, Luce?" Now Ben sounded impatient. "You've never been one for introspection."

"And you give a damn because?" Good, he actually flinched.

"Don't, Luce," he said. "Don't. We agreed. Keep it secret and without strings. I was happy with the arrangement. You're the one who broke it off."

She turned to face him. "I'm leaving. I'm going back to Portland."

Disappointment and something else – regret, anger? – flashed in his eyes.

"You know you can't do that."

"I can do whatever I please."

"What about your sons?"

Why, why, did I tell him about them? "They're my reason for leaving."

His fingers danced a tango up her arm. "Can't you think of another?"

Heat flooded her face. God damn you, Ben.

"I miss what we had."

"No you don't." She held his gaze. The roller coaster ride was over.

"You promised me a waltz, Lucinda."

She blinked. How long had Jackson been standing there?

"Have fun, you crazy kids," Ben said. "I'll mingle until it's time for our tango, Jackson."

Jackson took her arm and led her to the grassy dance floor. He surprised her by being a superb dancer. She felt weightless in his arms. She closed her eyes and pushed her bitter thoughts away. What harm in pretending, if only for a few hours, that she belonged to this picture-postcard evening?

# 18

"This is the last one," Carol said, placing a glass chimney over a lantern. She and Lorrie were in the kitchen readying lanterns for tables on the lawn.

Lorrie took off her apron and hung it on a peg. "Okay. Let's deliver these things and join the party." She picked up two lanterns and, using her hip to open the screen door, led the way outside. They stopped on the porch to watch Joe Wright, Winter's seventy-five-year-old beekeeper, blow an immense bubble through a plastic wand. The bubble shivered and broke free and the group surrounding him gasped, turning their faces up to follow its path as it soared over their heads and disappeared into the sycamore trees that dotted the lawn.

"Ben sure knows how to please children. Leave it to him to think of bringing bubble kits to the party."

"He knows how to please the young at heart, too," Carol said, nodding toward Joe.

At the bottom of the steps they ran into Will. Lorrie flashed him a grin and kept going. Before Carol could follow, Will placed his hand on her arm.

"I was looking for you. How about a dance?"

"I'm helping Lorrie right now. Besides, I'm not much of a dancer."

"I don't believe you." He took the lanterns from her hands. "I'm going to deliver these to their tables and come back for you. Be prepared to trip the light fantastic."

"Trip being the operative word, I'm afraid," Carol said.

After he walked off she smoothed her dress, a moss green, square-necked cotton velvet that deepened the color of her eyes and made her feel almost pretty, so long as she avoided mirrors. Funny, though, she found she no longer cared what the mirror said.

When Will returned, he took her hand. "Time to boogie."

Luce and Jackson waltzed by as they entered the dance floor, Luce looking fragile as spun glass in Jackson's huge arms. With her eyes closed and her mouth curved in a smile, she resembled a young girl enjoying her first prom.

Lorrie's raucous laughter rang out as Rick bent her in a deep dip, the two laughing so hard Carol expected them to collapse onto the grass.

She stumbled.

"Carol?"

"Yes?"

"I think you're supposed to pay attention to your partner."

"I'm sorry. I'm having way too much fun watching everyone else. Look, Joe Wright is dancing with Cora." Earlier, Carol had been shocked to see what age and disappointment had done to the attractive, if rather stern, woman she remembered. "And look at the Blue Hawks. They're amazing dancers."

Will swung her out, twirled her once and brought her back against him. It was the surprise, she decided, that made it possible for her to follow him. If she'd been expecting the move, she would have stumbled again for sure.

He twirled her again.

Carol couldn't believe it. Hot damn! I'm two for two.

"By the way," Will said, when they assumed a more sedate pace. "I really do need an extra hand. Have you thought at all about joining my crew?"

Startled, she stopped. Will didn't. His booted foot came down on her toes.

"Ouch!" she blurted, loud enough that several heads turned in their direction.

"I'm sorry. Did I hurt you?"

"No," she lied, seeing his stricken expression. "You know, Will, I have absolutely no experience in your line of work."

"Don't need any." Will began leading her again. "Nothing you don't do in your own yard." He spun her. "Did I mention a four-day week? Done by two every afternoon? Your own personal chauffeur, meaning me? I'd pick you up every morning and bring you home."

Why not? Time I got out more. The extra money won't hurt, either. "Give me a couple of days to think about it?"

He smiled down at her. "Sure."

Under his gaze Carol felt a strange sensation building inside. She didn't know whether to be sorry or relieved when the music ended and they separated to applaud the musicians.

A slender woman dressed in an ankle length denim skirt and a red peasant blouse passed them on her way to the musician's makeshift platform. Long, salt and pepper hair brushed her shoulders and several strands of colored beads glittered against her blouse. After a brief discussion with the musicians, she reached into her skirt and brought out a harmonica.

"Margaret Lawson," Will said. "She's been a fixture on the Portland jazz scene for years. Lucky for us she's visiting friends here."

The woman brought the instrument to her mouth. The haunting strains of "Ruby" floated into the night. Without hesitation or forethought, Carol moved into Will's arms. This time, she had no trouble following his lead.

*** 

Will parked the car and turned off the engine.

Carol wondered if driving her home had been his idea or Lorrie's. "Thanks for the ride, Will. I can see myself inside."

"I'm sure you can, but I'll walk you to the door anyway." He cuffed her lightly on the shoulder. "Can't have you putting too much weight on that trampled foot."

He took the key from her when they reached the door. "I'm not going to make a big deal out of this, Carol, but about those letters –"

"Don't, please, Will. It was so long ago."

"I want you to know how sorry I am for the hurt it caused you."

He didn't wait for her reply, but took her face in his hands, leaned down, and kissed her cheek. "Sleep well, Carol."

Inside the house, she brought her hand to her cheek. The kiss had been friendly, devoid of passion, but Will had placed it on the damaged side, finding it no different from the other. Humming "Ruby," she went to the kitchen to grind beans for her morning coffee and noticed the blinking red eye on the answering machine. Message. More likely two or three. In the last week she'd received sales pitches offering cruise tickets and low interest rates for refinancing the mortgage she didn't have. She pushed Play. An odd, hissing sound issued from the speaker. Her finger settled on the Delete key, but before she pressed, a woman's distinctive voice began a song Carol knew well. Her breath caught. Her hands flew out, sending the answering machine to the floor.

# 19

Not again. Breather phone calls, the buzzer sounding at one or three or five in the morning, taxi drivers or pizza delivery persons at the door, Malone smirking at work when only she could see him.

A laugh or a sob, she couldn't tell which, caught in her throat. At least in Winter she wouldn't have to worry about the taxis or pizza deliveries.

She'd been a fool to believe Malone would tire of harassing her. Instead, he escalated his campaign. Exhausted by this war without words, she had escaped to the coast for a weekend. She returned to an apartment in shambles, dishes smashed, favorite books soaking in bath water, feces smeared on the wall above her bed. Her clothes, her music collection, nothing escaped his rage. When she found Nina Simone's, *After Hours* CD floating in the toilet bowl, a CD they bought together, she knew he was responsible.

The police thought otherwise. "Random violence," they concluded. "Probably lucky you were gone when they broke in."

Two weeks later, her face freshly stitched back together, they reached a similar conclusion. Though she accused Malone in both instances, his alibis, confirmed by a female grad student, left her nowhere to turn.

Since her assailant wore a ski mask, Carol had to admit she hadn't seen his face. "But I heard his voice," she'd said.

"You were bleeding," one investigator said. "In shock. Confused."

Bleeding and in shock, yes. But not confused about the words hissed in her ear before she passed out. The same words Malone spoke the night she broke off with him, after he threw her against the wall: "I say when it's over."

Upstairs in bed, she stared through the windows at the star crowded sky. Of course he'd found her. The tin box he'd smashed had contained letters and cards from James. Letters he'd read before destroying, letters in envelopes with return addresses in the corner.

Fury, cold and hard as the blade of a knife, washed through her. Malone would not send her running again. She was tired of being a victim. Time she stood her ground. She leaped from the bed and began opening windows, hungry for fresh air. Back downstairs, she started coffee, picked the answering machine off the floor. Tomorrow she'd buy a new phone, one with caller ID.

When the coffee stopped perking she filled a heavy mug and took it to the table. She glanced at the clock, surprised by how much time had passed. Will should be up soon.

By seven, she could wait no longer. She found his number, dialed.

"Will?" she said, when he answered. "It's Carol. I'm taking you up on the job offer. I'm ready to begin working on Monday."

Her fingers tangled in the phone cord. She nodded, though she knew he couldn't see her.

"Of course I'm sure," she answered. "Monday."

# 20

"To summarize, you'll rake, mow, water, pull weeds, and plant," Will explained on their way to town Monday morning. "I'm partnering you with Sarah Roan Horse, Grace and Louis' niece. Gerry and I take care of the heavy work."

"Gerry?"

"Gerry Daniels. He's a student, like Sarah." Will took his eyes from the road and glanced at her. "Okay so far?"

"Got it."

Lady, head resting on Carol's knee, twitched in her sleep.

"I don't go many places without her," Will had said when she opened the pickup door and saw Lady sprawled on the seat.

She ran her hand over the dog's black coat, feeling the slick scars that crisscrossed her warm hide. Her own injuries had nearly healed, forming a network of white. Looking into the mirror that morning she decided the scars resembled an albino spider squashed under someone's heel. The flattened body sat on her cheek bone, the legs, broken and twisted, pointing every which way. One almost touched the outer corner of her eye, another her ear, while two stretched toward the side of her nose and corner of her mouth. Lovely. She pushed the image away with a sigh.

"You were going to be a teacher, Will. What happened?"

Will shifted gears as they approached the first of three railroad crossings. His eyes remained on the road. "Life."

Taking his terse reply as a warning, Carol settled into silence.

A few miles later, they rounded a bend, surprising a flock of red-winged blackbirds at the side of the road. They flew up, crimson feathers flashing beneath their wings. They settled a few yards away, into the wheat field adjoining the highway. Will took another sharp corner and hit the brakes. Three cows ambled down the center line toward them. Lady popped up, barking at the slow-moving beasts.

"Damn cows," Will said. "Gotta be a fence down somewhere." He navigated around the laconic animals, using his horn to herd them aside. "I like a good steak, but sometimes..."

In southeast Pendleton, he parked in front of a small, white bungalow with door, window frames, and flower boxes painted a dark green. Daffodils and narcissus grew thick in a border that separated yard from sidewalk. Across the front of the house, tulips of every color imaginable, red and orange, yellow, pink, burgundy and purple- some solid, some striped, made for a cheerful riot of color. Pots of ivy geranium with blooms striped pink and white filled the window boxes.

An elderly woman, her body so bent she resembled a question mark, came from the house to meet them. She wore a maroon cardigan over a blue and white housedress, support hose, and lace-up shoes with one inch heels.

Will placed his arm around her when he made introductions. "Wilma Reed, meet Carol Ingram, the newest member of our crew."

So many lines crossed the elderly woman's weathered face, it appeared carved from wood. Drooping lids nearly obscured faded blue eyes, but not the quick intelligence that shone in them. She reached for Carol's hand, her grip surprisingly strong.

"Welcome, Carol." Her bright eyes fixed on Will. "This one's too thin. She needs fattening."

"I'm not thin, just wiry," Carol joked.

Wilma's gravelly laugh put Carol in mind of smoky rooms and cut crystal glasses filled with amber liquid.

"Of course you are, dear," she said, "I knew that the moment I set eyes on you." She stepped between them and linked their arms with hers.

"Coffee cake's ready, where's that Sarah?"

"On her way," Will said. "She had to stop at the college to leave off a paper. Carol, get ready for a treat. Wilma makes the best coffee cake in town."

Wilma peered around Will and winked. "Crumb cake, Will's favorite."

*\*\*\**

Wilma was no little old lady with a basket of knitting sitting beside her rocking chair. For starters, she didn't have a rocking chair, or a basket of knitting. No-nonsense Swedish furniture mixed with antique oak pieces. Matted prints by Freda Kahlo hung on one wall. The arm of a moss green, camel-back sofa held a bright, multi-colored throw made of squares of velvet. Pottery, hand-woven baskets, and books spilled from bookcases built in on either side of a small, hand-tiled fireplace. Carol was about to ask if she could look at the books when the doorbell pealed.

"That will be our Sarah," Wilma said. "Open the door for her, please Will. She reached for Carol's arm and guided her to the dining room. "Sit. By the time Will and Sarah settle, I'll have the coffee cake on the table."

# 21

The four-day work week flew by, and when Friday arrived, Carol celebrated with a long soak in a lavender scented tub. Hiking over hills and working in her own yard and garden had conditioned her, but the work with Sarah had given her a few twinges to get rid of.

Looking down at her submerged body, she knew Wilma Reed had been right. She needed fattening. Though she had gained weight over the last weeks, she could still count her ribs. Twenty pounds had melted away during the last weeks in California.

Malone hadn't contacted her again. She wasn't fool enough to believe he'd finished with her. More likely he was congratulating himself for keeping her in suspense while he planned his next move. Funny though, once she decided to stand her ground, plus being with Will and Sarah and meeting Wilma, she hadn't given him much thought. Thinking of the elderly woman brought a smile. What a role model. Arthritis had crippled her body, but not her spirit. She exhibited more energy than people three times younger. And Sarah. Will had been right. She *was* a sweetheart.

Slender, copper-skinned and raven-haired, her flashing eyes and ready smile radiated good will. Who could resist such enthusiasm? Yesterday, on their lunch break, Sarah had opened the gold, oval locket that hung from her neck, to reveal a picture of a toddler with her bright eyes and smile.

"Brandon. He's four," she'd said, with obvious pride. "He's in Montana with my mom while I work toward my nursing degree."

Carol couldn't hide her surprise. "You're a mother?"

"I am. And Brandon is the best thing that ever happened to me. I was sixteen when he was born. Thought I was in love." She laughed. "My boyfriend wasn't ready to be a father. He sends money for Brandon when he can, but he didn't finish high-school, so finding work is hard. She snapped the locket shut. Her voice grew soft. "I miss my son like crazy but we have Thanksgiving, Christmas, and summers together. Once I get my degree, we'll be together for keeps. And we're lucky. We have family to support us. "

The cooling bath water brought Carol back to the present. She nudged the hot water tap on. A few more minutes soaking, then a real breakfast, orange juice, bacon, pancakes smothered in maple syrup, maybe even a couple of eggs, over-easy.

Wilma would approve.

\*\*\*

Bright blue flashed outside the French door. Carol recognized the jay that often showed up to wage war with a resident squirrel, both claiming the same tree branch for their own. She often wondered how the branch stayed intact, the way the two fought over it. She bit into her bacon, hearing the familiar angry squawk from the jay. The squirrel answered in kind, a staccato chatter filled with outrage. Smiling, she cut a generous wedge from her stack of pancakes, swirled it through a puddle of syrup, and had it halfway to her mouth when the phone rang. Ignoring the jump in her pulse, she waited for the answering machine to kick in, hoping to hear Lorrie's cheery voice, or another taped recording offering a mortgage payment deal. What she heard startled her.

"Carol? It's Will, guess you're not home…"

She pushed away from the table and grabbed the receiver.

"Sorry, Will, I was in the middle of something. What's up?"

"I don't mean to interrupt your down time – "

"You want me to work today," she finished. "Give me twenty minutes."

His laugh cut her off.

"Heck, no, I'm inviting you to a barbecue at my place, hot dogs, hamburgers, potato salad and cheap beer. The usual suspects are coming, also Sarah, her aunt and uncle, and Dave Linfield, a deputy sheriff friend of ours who's dating Sarah."

"Sounds like fun. What should I bring?"

"Yourself. Luce and I have this one covered."

"What time?"

"Say around four?"

"Perfect. I'll see you then."

After Carol put the phone down, she gazed out the window, lost in thought. She had come-- no, she had run--here to hide, not only from Malone, but from what she had become because of him. Was it only weeks ago she dressed in suits and sat behind a desk all day? Now she wore jeans and pulled weeds, and felt more alive than she had in years. Old friends had welcomed her return without question or condemnation. If she hadn't been truthful about her 'accident,' she rationalized the omission by telling herself the truth didn't matter. She knew if Malone ever did come after her, her fragile house of cards would collapse. But she couldn't worry about that now. Her life was on track again. She would do whatever necessary to keep it that way.

# 22

At first, Carol thought she'd taken a wrong turn and arrived at the wrong house. The standard white box with black painted shutters and cramped front porch that she remembered from visits with her uncle no longer existed. In its place stood a house of midnight blue with shutters painted persimmon, and instead of a porch, sported a three-sided deck, both roofed and railed.

Seeing Ben and Will's vehicles reassured her. A hornet yellow, older model Chevrolet – good grief, was that a raccoon tail hanging off the antenna? – she guessed belonged to a lanky, sandy-haired man on the deck. Carol got out of the car and started up the walk. She reached the deck as the man, wearing khaki shorts and a short-sleeved shirt printed with beer labels, pulled a frosted bottle of beer from an ice chest. He grinned, snagged a second beer and popped the caps. "Ladies first," he said, handing the first one over.

"Thanks," she said, taking the ice cold bottle in hand. "You must be Dave."

"Busted." The skin around his eyes crinkled with his smile. Nice eyes, Carol noted, hazel with tiny flecks of gold. Nice smile, too. Sarah hadn't mentioned him, but it was easy to imagine the two of them together. He didn't appear too much older than her either, maybe twenty-three or twenty-four to her twenty.

"The raccoon tail is a fake, in case you were wondering."

She laughed. "Now I'm busted."

She was aware of his scrutiny, but found she didn't mind. Second nature, she imagined, for someone in police work.

"You must be Carol. How do you like working for a slave driver like Will?"

"He's okay when he isn't using the whip."

Dave took a long swallow of beer, wiped his mouth with the back of his hand and let out a sigh. "Man, nothing beats the first taste."

Carol took a decent swallow of hers. "You're right. Nothing like it." She looked around. "Where are the others?"

"In back, checking out the grill. Rick and Lorrie should be here soon, and Sarah and her aunt and uncle." He grinned. "That's why I'm here. I'm waiting for Sarah."

Carol was about to mention how much she enjoyed Sarah's company when his attention strayed over her shoulder and his face lit up. "Here comes Sarah now."

Carol turned as Sarah's small pickup entered the driveway.

"I'll go say hello to our hosts," she said. I'll see you later."

"Sure," he said, his gaze still on Sarah. "Later."

Carol followed a flagstone path to the back of the house and found Ben, Jackson and Will on the patio studying a gas grill as though they'd found the Holy Grail, only to find it wanting.

Ben was the first to notice her arrival. "Hey, here's our girl. Good to see you again, Carol."

Jackson raised his hand in greeting.

Will gestured toward the grill. "Seems I forgot to check the propane tank. It's empty."

"I like my hamburgers medium, Will, not raw," Carol said.

Jackson snickered.

"Not to worry," Will said. "I have my faithful Weber."

As though on cue, Luce walked toward them from a small storage shed, a bag of charcoal in her hands. She dropped it at Ben's feet and brushed gray powder from her hands.

Jackson whipped a handkerchief from his back pocket and offered it to her.

"Thanks, Jackson, glad to see one gentleman here," Luce said, her tone good-natured.

Ben coughed into his hand – or was he laughing? Carol wasn't sure.

"Why don't you get the Weber from the shed and start the charcoal?"

"Your every wish is my command, Princess." Ben said. He leaned toward her and used his thumb to wipe a smudge of charcoal from her cheek. "Her highness has a dirty face."

Ignoring him, Luce took Jackson's hand. "Come help in the kitchen, Big J. You can press burgers while I slice tomatoes and onions. Will, why don't you give Carol a quick tour of the house?"

Ben watched Luce and Jackson leave, shaking his head in mock despair. "Poor Jackson, talk about leading a lamb to slaughter."

Will grinned. "Or the other way around. There's more to Jackson than size." He took Carol's arm. "Come on, I'll give you the cook's tour."

Carol's second surprise came inside the house. Gone the heavy drapes and overstuffed furniture, the dark wool rugs she remembered. The bare floors were polished oak, the living room furnishings spare, a camel-backed sofa, an old-fashioned easy chair, and an antique oak sewing rocker. Natural bamboo shaded the windows and the built-in bookcase that covered one wall held photographs and personal items as well as books. A trio of black and white photographs, simply framed, hung on one wall. Carol walked closer to view them: an owl on a post, a full moon reflected in its eyes; a winter pond ringed by snow-capped stones; a stand of aspens, bare branches like calligraphy against a leaden sky.

"These are beautiful, Will. I didn't know you were a photographer."

"I'm not. I just enjoy taking pictures. Come on, I'll show you the kitchen."

Luce and Jackson worked together at an island, Jackson forming hamburger patties while Luce arranged tomato, onion and lettuce slices on a platter. Carol gasped when she saw the restaurant-sized, stainless steel oven. "Wow," she whispered.

"Real men like to cook," Will quipped.

He took her back through the living room and down a hall. "Luce's room," he said, pointing to a closed door. He passed a bathroom, stopped at the next door. "My office, such as it is." Carol glimpsed a neat room containing a shelved unit with a printer, computer tower, monitor and keyboard. On another wall a bookcase, with titles on landscaping, sprinkler systems, even outdoor lighting. Drawers on a file cabinet were labeled. She saw the word, *Invoices* on the top drawer before they moved on. At the end of the hall, two more doors. "Utility room on the left," Will said. He opened the opposite door. "My bedroom."

A platform bed covered with tan duvet faced a window, a double chest of drawers, surface bare but for three, silver-framed photographs. A Hiroshige print hung on the wall opposite the bed. Here again, bamboo blinds took the place of curtains.

She walked to over to the dresser to look at the photos.

"My wife, Jordan," Will said, picking one up and handing it to her.

Carol studied the picture. "She's beautiful, Will. I was so sorry to hear what happened. I should have said something earlier, about your mom, too, but I wasn't sure how – "

"No words necessary, Carol." He took the photo from her and placed it back on the dresser.

"Come on, let's join the others."

# 23

"Will's done a great job on the house, hasn't he?" Ben said

"He sure has," Carol said. "I barely recognize the place."

Louis Blue Hawk, a barrel-chested man with a shock of white hair, rose to his feet at her approach and extended his hand.

"Call me Lou," he'd said the night of Rick and Lorrie's party. His wife, Grace, smiled a hello. Grace had the same slender form and liquid black eyes as her niece, but her hair was silver, worn today in a thick braid that fell over one shoulder.

"Hi Louis, hi Grace," Carol said. "Boy, Grace, it's easy to see where Sarah gets her looks."

Grace's smile grew even wider, revealing deep dimples. "How nice of you to say so," she said, "but you should see her mama."

Jackson and Luce came outside as Dave, holding hands with Sarah, called, "Here come the Donfield's."

All eyes went to the red Miata coasting to a stop near the walk. Lorrie jumped from the driver's side, hair catching the sun and sparking like copper wire. She ran around to the passenger side and opened the door for Rick, who emerged with a disgruntled expression and a pie in each hand. The boys untangled themselves from the rear, raced to the deck, and after polite hellos, raided the ice chest for cokes.

Carol thought Jackson's expression hilarious as his eyes traveled from the pies in Rick's hands to his pursed lips. His big chest rumbled with laughter.

Rick let his shoulder slump. He shook his head. "What's wrong with this picture?"

"Ignore him, everyone," Lorrie said. "He's upset because men drive, they don't carry pies.'" She took one from him and handed it off to Will. "Here. I don't trust my husband to balance two things at once."

Lorrie exchanged greetings with everyone, giving Sarah a quick hug. "We haven't seen you in ages. Will working you too hard?"

Sarah's skin turned rosy. "I've been busy studying for finals."

Carol was sliding a chair toward Lorrie when she noticed a seated figure under the cottonwood tree at the edge of Will's yard.

"Will, is that Cora?"

He nodded. "Ben brought her. She agreed to come if we left her in peace. She likes that spot, comes here by herself now and then to sit there. Kind of spooked me at first, but I guess she's remembering better times."

"I'm going to say hello."

"She'll bite your head off," Lorrie warned.

"We better get these pies inside," Will said to Rick. "By the way, partner, did you know a hint of vanilla does wonders for apple pie? I'd be happy to share my recipe with you."

Rick punched him in the arm with his free hand. "Vanilla, my ass," he said.

\*\*\*

"Remember me, Mrs. Newsome, Carol, James Fuller's niece? We didn't get a chance to talk at Rick and Lorrie's party." Cora glanced up and her mouth thinned. Carol felt her good intentions wilt under the woman's baleful stare. Though time and bitterness had treated her with cruel indifference, the talcum powder scent that rose from her gaunt body was one Carol remembered well.

"Can I bring you something cold to drink, Coke, Seven Up?"

"Nothing, thanks. I'm perfectly happy here, where I don't have to watch Jackson and that cheap slut Will gives house room to."

Carol took an involuntary step back, shocked by the venom in Cora's remark.

The woman's tongue snaked out and wet her lips. "Jackson's too quiet, always pussy-footin' around with those birds of his." She folded her arms across her flat chest. "And that Lucinda Frye? Trash. One look is all anyone needs to know that about her. I can't believe Will brought her here to my house."

Carol decided against a reply. Nothing she said would change Cora's mindset. She made one last attempt at politeness. "Sure I can't bring you anything?"

Did Cora's expression soften the slightest bit?

"Well, I guess, if you wouldn't mind too much, I could do with a Coke."

"Sure."

Lorrie, sitting beside Grace on the deck, met Carol's return with raised eyebrows.

"She wants a Coke," Carol explained, and took one from the ice chest. She returned to Cora and opened the tab before handing it over.

Cora took a sip, nodded. "Thank you, Carol. Now, please, go join the others. I'm fine where I am."

Carol hesitated, but the set of the Cora's jaw warned her. This elderly Cora wasn't any different from the tightly-wound younger one Carol remembered. She hadn't smiled much then, either, unless her husband was with her. Only around him had she seemed human. No wonder she shut down after he left.

\*\*\*

Alone, Cora gazed at the tree where the initials, RN + CN, were carved into the trunk, the word, always, carved below them. Roger had done that the day they moved into the house.

A ripple of laughter drifted from the deck. Cora's mouth twisted.

"You goddamn fool, Roger," she hissed. "That should be us, having our neighbors over. You threw our future away, all because I said I didn't want children to come between us. My love suffocated you, that's what you said." The coke slipped from her hand and fell to the ground. She sat, unmindful, as yellow-jackets, drawn by the sweet spill, swarmed over the mouth of the can.

# 24

Saturday morning, Carol sang in the shower. She'd had a wonderful time at Will's barbecue, though a few awkward moments came at the table when Cora pointedly ignored Jackson's attempts at conversation. He appeared hurt and confused by her attitude. Not Luce, who had stared pointedly at Cora with an amused smile.

Carol dressed in jeans and cotton sweater, filled a large mug with coffee, and carried it down to the creek. Settled on a flat rock, she drank her coffee and enjoyed the scenery. The water, a burnished silver, smelled faintly metallic. A southerly breeze riffled the pines, and overhead, cottonwoods and alders conversed in soft whispers. Later, she'd work in her vegetable garden. She'd harvested peas, spring onions, and lettuce. If all went well, she'd have broccoli, beets, squash, green beans, and tomatoes later in the season. Just thinking about a homegrown tomato, picked from the vine, still warm from the sun and sprinkled with salt, made her mouth water. She hadn't eaten tomatoes that way since summers with James.

\*\*\*

On Monday when she walked outside to wait for Will, she found an intricate web spun between the gate posts, each lucent strand pearled with dew. The finest Belgium lace couldn't compete with the arachnid's art. She ducked under the web, careful to avoid disturbing the maker, a beautiful, emerald green spider still at work in one corner. Will pulled in few moments later. She climbed into the pickup, nodded at Will, and patted Lady's head. Lady responded by nuzzling Carol's neck before she settled back down.

Sarah and a stocky young man with spiked brown hair waited at the curb when they arrived at Wilma's. Lady barked on seeing them, and when Will let her out of the pickup, she danced around both, emitting joyful yips.

"Carol, meet Gerry Adler," Will said. "Watch him. While he's charming you with stories – none of them true, I might add - he'll be snitching your share of coffeecake."

Gerry grinned. "He's jealous because I'm the better story-teller." He thrust his hand out. "Nice meeting you, Carol." A gold hoop pierced one ear, and a tiny dragon tattoo decorated his left bicep. Before she could remark on the dragon, Wilma came from the house, this time using a cane as she made her way toward them. She pulled Gerry into a tight, one-arm embrace. "Missed you last week," she said, and with the throaty laugh Carol loved, took his arm. "Coffee cake's out of the oven. Will, if you don't mind, I'll ask you to serve while Gerry pours our coffee. My damn hip is giving me fits today."

Thirty minutes later, coffee cake demolished, Will and Gerry cleared the table, kissed Wilma on both cheeks, and left for jobs on the south side of town. Carol and Sarah washed the dishes, and after seeing Wilma comfortably settled with a book, went out to work in her yard. This time, Sarah mowed and watered while Carol weeded, finding more weeds this time, proof that Wilma's hip had kept her from the work she loved. How did she manage housekeeping when her arthritis flared up? Carol wondered if she'd be insulted by an offer to help with that. She'd mention it to Will later.

At the Milbank's, Dan Milbank followed them around as he had before. At one point, Carol turned and caught him watching Sarah. In that unguarded moment, his thoughts were clear, and not at all pretty. Carol stared at him, willing him to notice. When he did, he flushed a deep red and retreated to his house where he remained for the rest of their stay. Another thing to bring up with Will. Sarah should never work here alone.

# 25

On their way back to Winter, Carol broached the subject of Wilma.

"That's nice of you, Carol, but she has a granddaughter who comes in to help when necessary. I know because I worried about the same thing, so I asked."

"Okay, one problem solved. Now I'll give you another." She paused, not quite sure how to begin, decided to just dive in. "Dan Milbank."

"Overweight guy with beady eyes who letches after Sarah?"

Carol punched Will's arm. "You know. Why didn't you say something?"

"No need. He's a creep. I never leave her alone with him. In fact, Sarah – or you if Sarah can't make it – will never be left on your own where a male client under eighty is on the premises." Will's right hand left the steering wheel long enough to stroke Lady's back. "Satisfied?"

"Yes, thank you."

They were passing through Thornhollow now, the Umatilla River a ribbon of blue on their left.

"I've picked up three new clients," Will announced. "I think we can handle the extra work without losing our three-day weekend if we add an extra hour or so to our afternoons. Would you mind?"

"Not at all. Congratulations, Will." Carol enjoyed everything about her work, including the commute. Who wouldn't enjoy seeing the river turn gold in the morning sun, or the wildflowers that shimmered on the hills like a Monet landscape? What a contrast to her California commute, where crowded freeways and frustrated drivers were the norm, and gridlock an almost daily occurrence. No exhaust fumes, if you didn't count getting behind the occasional vintage truck, and no white knuckle driving caused by tailgaters threatening to run you off the road. "But can three of us cope? When spring term ends, Sarah's off to Montana."

"Sarah might stay on a while longer."

She glanced at him. "Really? She talks nonstop about seeing Brandon again."

"True, but if she goes to summer school she earns her nursing degree a semester sooner. She wanted to check with her mom before she decided. Her mother said go for it."

Lady lifted her head from Will's leg, dropped it down again.

Carol patted the dog's rump. "I'm selfish enough to say I'm glad. I was missing her before she even left." She meant it, too.

Happiness flowed from Sarah like water from a tap and was contagious. Last Thursday, she'd gotten tangled in a garden hose and fell face down in a muddy puddle. She'd come up howling with laughter and had refused to wash the mud from her face until they finished the job. "I'd pay a fortune at a salon for this," she'd said. "Why not take advantage of a good thing?" Since then, Carol called her Sarah Sunbeam, much to the girl's amusement.

A moment later they were crossing Sorrow Creek Bridge. A car and three pickups were parked on the grass verge above the creek, a popular spot because fishermen could wade into the creek from there with ease. Only one angler, wearing a dark green hat, was visible. The others must have moved up or downstream to favorite holes.

"Good day for fishing," Will said. He pulled up to her mailbox so she could check for mail. "Think I'll give Ben a call when I get home, see if he wants to go out later."

Carol reached through the window, opened the box and retrieved an advertising circular addressed to Occupant, and a western-wear catalog bearing her uncle's name.

When they reached the house, Lady's muzzle went up. Her good ear cocked and a low whine vibrated in her chest.

"Oh-oh," Carol said with a grin. "Guess who wants a rematch?"

Last week, Lady had leaped from the truck the minute Carol opened the door. A hilarious chase after a squirrel followed. The quick-footed rodent had been the hands-down winner, giving Lady chattering hell from the safety of a tree. What had driven

Carol to body-hugging laughter though, was Will's red face when he had to drag Lady, stiff-legged as a taxidermist's dream, back to his truck.

The whine changed to a rumble.

"Better hold her, Will, or we'll have a repeat of last week."

Will grasped her collar. "I'll restrain Cujo while you get out."

Carol stifled a laugh. "Good luck."

She rolled up the window before she let herself out and shut the door quickly behind her. Will let go of Lady's collar and she sprang at the window, paws scrabbling against the glass. Her frantic barking continued, even after Will drove out of sight.

Jet streams crisscrossed the sky over the ridge. A Monarch butterfly floated toward her, landed on the fence and flexed its brilliant wings before flying off again.

A perfect day, but at the gate she saw that the web had been torn, slender filaments hanging from both posts, the weaver nowhere to be seen.

She understood why when Tom Malone stepped from the side of the house and started toward her.

# 26

She backed away from the gate, keeping her gaze locked on him. In spite of herself, her heart kicked into overdrive, batting against her chest like a trapped bird.

His attack in the parking lot had been swift, so unexpected she'd had no time for fear. One minute she was unlocking her car door, the next, she was on her back on the asphalt, the weight of his body pinning her down, a map of fire drawn on her face with broken glass. Disbelief, not fear, had gripped her until the moment she passed out.

"You're trespassing, Tom," she said, unable to keep a tremor from her voice.

He heard it and his lips twitched. "Gosh, sweetheart, aren't you glad to see me?" He smiled – a smile so open, so free of guile – that for an incredible moment, Carol almost returned it.

He could have modeled for L.L. Bean or J.R. Crew with his all-American looks, blond hair styled to look disheveled, sea-glass-blue eyes, and standing a little over six feet. Dressed in pressed khaki slacks and navy polo shirt with a little alligator embossed on the breast pocket, he looked every inch the respectable young professional he wanted others to see, and see him they did. She'd learned that soon enough. Even her boss, the Dean, had taken Tom's protestations of innocence to heart.

The coldness in his eyes told a different story.

"I doubt your boss would understand your coming here, especially after you convinced him that I was the one with a problem."

His hand gripped the gate, his smile widening. "But I'm not here. I'm attending a seminar in Portland, several hundred miles from here. My friend will confirm it. You remember her, the grad student I was tutoring the night your luck ran out?" He cocked his head to one side, studying her. "Too bad," he drawled. "You used to be almost pretty."

She fought an urge to throw up. "Forget your ski mask?"

"Didn't think I'd need one in the boonies, sweetheart."

How far could she run before he caught her? No one would hear her scream. She scanned the ground for a rock, a stick, anything to protect herself. Nothing but dirt.

"And what in God's name have you done to your hair? Looks like you took a lawnmower to it."

When they dated he insisted she could never cut it.

"You're smart, figure it out." No tremor in her voice now. Even the smallest creature fights when cornered.

Her defiance triggered his fury. He barreled through the gate and sent her sprawling. She got her nails on his face before he captured her hands.

"You bitch," he said, his tone so lacking in feeling he might have been commenting on the weather. "How am I supposed to explain the scratches?" He leaned down. Hot breath laced with alcohol brushed her face. "I have to admit, you surprise me. I didn't think you had any fight left."

She squirmed beneath him, pulled a hand free, and clawed his forearm.

His fist shot out.

Blood filled her mouth. The sky over his shoulders began to spin, a blue vortex, sucking her in.

"Relax, baby," he purred, his hands tugging the waistband of her jeans. "Might as well enjoy this, I know I'm going –" He screamed and tumbled from her body. "Carol, call this animal off me!"

She struggled to her feet and saw Malone on his back, Lady standing over him, teeth bared and only inches from his throat. Will was back, too, though she hadn't heard him arrive. He probed her scalp with his fingers. She tasted blood and thought she might throw up.

"Thank God for a smart dog," Will said. "Lady made such a fuss I stopped at the end of the road and let her out. She took off like a shot. Took me a minute to turn the pickup around." He held three fingers before her eyes. "Don't laugh. I need you to tell me how many fingers you see."

She did laugh. Such a cliché. "Six," she said, just to rattle him. She couldn't believe she was treating this so lightly. Maybe having her worst fear realized, and surviving, had something to do with it. "I'm joking. Three. Honest, Will, I'm okay."

"Do you know this guy?"

Carol nodded. "Afraid so." She couldn't hold back her satisfaction when she saw a wet stain spreading over the crotch of Tom's no-longer-perfectly-creased slacks.

Will called Lady, who retreated, still growling. Malone got to his feet.

"You've got it all wrong, man. I came to see an old friend and," he sent a wary glance at Lady, "your crazy dog misunderstood." He smiled with the confidence of a man used to charming everyone in his path.

A smile that had no effect because Will's punch sent him staggering.

Malone stayed on his feet. Massaging his jaw, he tried another smile. "Hey, I know what it looks like but Carol and I go way back. She likes it rough – or maybe you already know that." He leered. "Gosh, sweetheart, guess you didn't waste any time jumping into the sack with someone else."

Will's foot shot out. Malone's screamed and doubled over. An object fell from his pocket, glinting in the light. He reached for it but Will was faster. Carol heard a click before Will held it up for her to see.

A switchblade.

# 27

Carol stared at the knife for a moment before she pushed past Will and faced Malone. "What, no broken bottle this time?"

She heard Will's sharp intake of breath. "Carol, do you want to call the sheriff or should I?

"I'll call."

She did more than call. She washed her face and hands and ran a comb through her hair before she rejoined Will. "Dave's sending two men. They should be here in about fifteen minutes."

They heard the sirens coming long before two cruisers reached them. Each deputy came from their vehicle with hands resting on the holstered guns at their sides.

Within minutes, Tom was handcuffed and hustled, protesting, into one vehicle, and driven away.

The remaining deputy approached them, notebook in hand. He nodded at Will but spoke to Carol. "I'm Deputy Baldwin, Miss Ingram. Sheriff McReady says you need to see a doctor."

Carol shook her head. "I told him I didn't need one. I'm fine, just a little shaken." She remembered her last emergency room visit, the questions and knowing looks. She wasn't going through that again. Nothing was broken, and nothing needed stitching. She hurt, but she would deal with the pain on her own.

Baldwin sighed. "I can't force you, of course, but the sheriff is going to read me the riot act for not convincing you." He took a pen from his pocket. "Okay if I ask you a few questions?"

"His name is Tom Malone," Carol said. "We dated in California. When I broke it off, he began stalking me. He trashed my apartment one weekend when I was out of town. Later, he attacked me in a parking lot and cut my face." She took a deep breath and forced the rest out. "You should know he had an alibi both times. No one believed me when I said he was responsible."

Will took her arm. "Baldwin, can't the rest wait? She's had a rough go. She needs rest."

The deputy snapped his notebook shut and put it in his back pocket. "I've got enough for now, Miss Ingram. Make sure you come into the department tomorrow. We'll need more details and photos of your injuries to accompany the arrest report, or the judge might decide there isn't enough evidence to support the charges. I'd hate to see this guy walk."

"I'll see that she gets there," Will said. "Thanks."

Baldwin pointed his thumb over his shoulder, back toward the road. "Looks like Malone parked at the bridge then walked here and hid behind the house until you came home. We'll send a tow truck out for the car."

"Thank God for Lady," Will said.

Baldwin chuckled. "Lady made our suspect wet himself. Jim's not happy about carrying him in his cruiser."

"She wanted to tear his throat out," Will said. "I was tempted to let her."

"Understandable, but not recommended." The deputy gave a brief salute. "I'll see you two later."

After Baldwin drove off, Will walked Carol to the house, his mind churning.

A broken bottle.

Jesus wept! He couldn't wrap his head around it.

# 28

While Carol fixed an ice pack for her mouth, Will called Lorrie. Moments later she arrived still wearing an apron. She took one look at Carol, braced her hands on her hips, and shook her head in disgust. "Aren't you a lovely sight? And Will says you won't see a doctor. Okay, tough one, let's get you cleaned up. Then we can decide about the doctor."

Carol removed the ice from her mouth. "I'm fine, just a little stiff."

"I'm going to start you a bath," Lorrie said. "Will, why don't you and Lady take a little walk?"

After Will and Lady left, she helped Carol undress. When and she saw the mottled bruises on her breasts and stomach, Lorrie exploded. "Goddamn that man to hell! Will should have tied the bastard to a fence post until I got here. Five minutes with me and he'd sing soprano for the rest of his unnatural life!"

She settled Carol into the tub, left, and returned with a glass of red wine.

"One glass won't hurt," she said, placing it in Carol's hand. "I'll stay close. Call if you need me."

"Lorrie?" Carol spoke in a whisper.

"Yes?"

"I'm sorry."

Lorrie sat on the edge of the tub. "What do you mean, you're sorry? You didn't do anything. This wasn't your fault."

"I'm sorry I lied." Carol touched her face. "Malone did this, not a car accident. It's why I came to Winter. I thought I'd be safe here."

"You are safe here. That bastard will never hurt you again."

"I lied about my job, too. I left California in the middle of the night without telling anyone. There is no job."

"I'm glad. That means you're staying here where you belong." Lorrie turned to leave, stopped. "Drink your wine. I'm going to heat some soup."

Carol took a cautious sip, winced when the liquid passed her cut lips. She set the glass down, leaned her head back against the rim of the tub, and closed her eyes. Lorrie had made confession easy but her kindness couldn't deafen the words that echoed in her head, Malone's words, chosen for maximum humiliation: "She likes it rough...already jumped in the sack with someone else..."

Carol shivered, cold in spite of the steaming water.

What must Will think?

\*\*\*

"You aren't spending the night, Lorrie, and that's final."

After the bath, wine, and the chicken soup she was now finishing, Carol could barely keep her eyes open.

"What if you wake up and need something?"

"I'm not going to wake up. I'll sleep like the dead after I finish this soup."

Lorrie snorted. "That may prove prophetic."

Carol lowered her spoon. "First, I'm fine. Really. Sore but nothing's broken. Second, Lor, I can't thank you enough, but honestly, all I want now is bed." She used her spoon to point. "You were wearing that apron when you got here. I hope you didn't leave a burner on."

Lorrie's pantomimed amazement. "What, you didn't hear the fire engines while you lazed in the tub?" She slipped the apron off and folded it. "Don't worry. I called Rick and the boys. Everything's under control."

"Good. Now go home to your family, Lorrie."

"After I get you settled."

Carol put her spoon in the bowl and stood. Will, listening to their exchange, joined Lorrie in helping Carol up the stairs. At her bedroom door he said goodnight and left.

"Sleep tight," Lorrie whispered, after she tucked Carol in. "I'll check with you tomorrow."

"I'm working tomorrow," Carol murmured, without opening her eyes.

"You're kidding."

"No, I'm not. Tell Will to pick me up at the usual time, or I'll go downstairs and tell him myself."

"Bet you change your mind come morning, but I'll tell him."

Carol was free-falling into deep space when Will's raised voice found its way upstairs.

"Is she nuts?"

# 29

A gargoyle stared from the mirror. Carol stared back at every child's nightmare, including her own.

Maybe styling her hair would help?

"Fat chance," she said, but reached for the curling iron anyway.

She had found Lorrie's note propped on the bedside table when she woke.

Will coming in morning BUT he agrees with me. You're nuts!!!

The dots beneath Lorrie's exclamation points had scowling faces drawn inside them.

Lorrie and Will. They had watched her yesterday as though any moment she might collapse. Lorrie wanted to spend the night, Will probably thought about it. They didn't understand her need to be alone, to prove to herself she had come through this, battered and bruised maybe, but intact, a survivor. And if she woke, screaming, like she did after Tom cut her face, she wanted no witnesses. She had very little pride left after yesterday but she intended to hang onto what remained. That meant showing a calm exterior, regardless of the turmoil raging inside.

She wrapped a section of hair around the hot iron and noticed her hands. They were shaking. She steadied herself against the vanity as tremors coursed under her skin.

Dammit! Taking a deep breath, she straightened her shoulders. She'd made it this far, she wasn't going to crumble now.

A few moments later she unplugged the curling iron and studied the results.

Crap!

Carol winced with each sip of coffee. A knock at the door made her jump. Coffee splashed over the cup rim and onto the table top.

Will stood on the porch.

"I'm fine," she said, before he could ask. "And you're early. I need a minute to fill my thermos."

"Sarah and Gerry are partnering this morning," Will said. "We're going to the sheriff's department to finish your complaint."

"Damn it, Will. I said I'm fine. We can do the complaint after work."

"Fine?" Disbelief coated his words. "Excuse me lady, how long ago did that truck run over you?"

"That's mean," she said, trying not to smile. "And beneath you, I might add."

He grinned. "I know." He checked his watch. "I told Dave we'd be there at eight. That leaves plenty of time for you to invite me in and offer me coffee."

Carol had never seen Will look smug before.

***

"Gosh darn-pardon-my-French, but he sure did a number on you," Dave blurted. Then he blushed. "Sorry, it's just that --"

"It's okay Dave," she said. "My exact thought when I faced the mirror this morning."

"Follow me, Carol. Not you, Will. 'fraid you'll have to enjoy the lack of comfort here in our waiting room. I'd offer you a cup of coffee, but the stuff Ron brewed this morning tastes like tar."

Dave led her down a hall and into a room painted pea-green. A sagging Venetian blind covered a single window behind a gray metal desk, bare but for a blotter and telephone. He waited until she took seat in cracked leather chair the color of mud before he dropped into the swivel chair behind the desk. His weight caused the chair to creak and tilt to one side.

Dave rolled his eyes. "County budget. We don't get too many perks here."

His expression grew serious. "Now, here's how this works. Malone's in the county jail. His initial court appearance will be in the next two or three days. At that time, the judge will inform him of the charge and make him aware of his rights." Dave's chair groaned as he leaned back and folded his hands over his stomach. "He's being charged with a felony, that switchblade was a big mistake. Because it's a felony charge he'll then be advised of his right to a preliminary hearing, the purpose of such a procedure, and his right to trial."

Carol gripped the arms on her chair. "Do I have to be there?"

Dave's chair squawked as he leaned forward. "No. That's Baldwin's responsibility. The victim rarely appears at a prelim but the arresting officer has to be there."

He reached into a drawer and pulled out several forms, pushing them toward Carol. "We need these completed. Let me know if you have any questions."

For the next few minutes the only sound in the room was the whisper of the ball point pen in Carol's hand, moving over the page.

A knock came at the door. It opened a crack and a female deputy poked her head into the room.

Dave nodded. "Come on in, Eve, we're almost done here." He turned to Carol. "This is Deputy Harding. She's going to photograph your injuries." He pushed back from the desk and stood up. "So, this Malone's a college professor?"

"Assistant professor," Carol corrected. "On a fast track to full tenure. He's very popular."

"So was Wayne Gacy until they found those bodies in his basement," he said. "The only fast track Malone is on now is the one to jail. He'll be popular there too, only not in quite the same way." He folded his arms. "A couple of things you should know. First, Malone could get bail at the initial hearing. He could even be released on his own recognizance, which I doubt, since he's from out of state. Second, I've started looking into his background. I'd bet my badge he's been in trouble before.

"Thanks, Dave." Carol said. She turned to Eve. "I'm ready."

Eve Harding led Carol to a small room with white walls and no window. "The scars on your face look recent," she said. "What happened?"

"I was attacked in California," Carol said. "Same guy, but I couldn't prove it."

"Well, you shouldn't have any trouble proving what he did this time. You have a witness."

Harding took several shots of Carol in full face and in profile. "What about your torso, any bruises?"

Carol raised her shirt. "Yes, but do we have to?"

"No time for modesty, Ms. Ingram. This is evidence."

# 30

Will rose from his chair when Carol re-appeared. "You look tired," he said. "And hungry. How about getting something to eat?"

"I'm not hungry. I thought we'd go to work after I filed the complaint."

Will shrugged. "Well, I am. Hungry, I mean. Someone was too lazy to offer me breakfast this morning. All that coffee sloshing around my insides is making me seasick."

"You're beginning to sound a lot like Rick."

His grin reached all the way to his ears. "I'll take that as a compliment."

Will's teasing did more to heal her spirit than any medicine. After yesterday, she feared what she might find in his eyes.

They ate at the Rainbow Café, a popular spot tucked between buildings on Main Street. Inside, an aisle separated high wooden booths on the left from the polished bar on the right. They walked past both to a large room in back and seated themselves at a table. When the waitress came, they ordered hash browns, scrambled eggs with ham, toast and coffee. Carol hadn't realized how hungry she was until she started eating. She looked up once, her mouth full of egg, and saw Will staring at her with amusement.

"Okay, you were right. This was a great idea. Thanks for suggesting it."

After breakfast, outside on the walk, he took his cell phone out. "I want to check in with Gerry and Sarah," he said and punched in a number. "Hey Gerry. Will here. How's it going? Uh huh. You're sure? Good. I'll be in touch."

He closed the phone and slid it back into his pocket. "Everything's under control. I'm taking you home."

Carol opened her mouth to argue, but Will's hand came up, cutting her off.

"No sass from you. Today, we're both taking a break. Tomorrow you can drag your aching body back to the salt mines. Believe me, I won't offer a word of sympathy."

Carol remained silent on their way back to his pickup, but when he opened the door and she struggled to climb into the seat without groaning, she admitted that a day's rest sounded a lot better than a day of weeding.

When they reached her place, Will helped her out. She stifled a moan when her feet touched the ground. His lips twitched but he remained blessedly mute.

"I'll be better tomorrow," she managed.

"No you won't," he said, his voice kind. "The first couple of days are always the worst. I've been there too, remember?"

Of course she did. The scar that bisected his eyebrow, the broken nose, and the bruises he wore when they were kids, all due to his stepfather, Ray.

She wasn't prepared for what he said next.

"After Jordan died, I did things, used people, in ways I'd rather not remember." He reached for a wayward lock of her hair and tucked it in place. "Don't beat yourself up over Malone. He's the past. Let it go."

He walked her to the front door, leaned down, and planted a light kiss to the south of her mouth. "I'll see you tomorrow."

"Thanks, Will," she said, and let herself inside before she made a complete fool of herself by bursting into tears.

# 31

Will's mood was considerably lighter driving home. Carol was bruised and sore, but when he thought about what might have been... She was safe now, facing a couple of rough days while her body healed, but safe. Her state of mind worried him more than her physical injuries, but she'd made it clear she intended to deal with that in her own way. He had to respect that.

Almost home. In another hour he'd be at the river. He'd give Ben a call. They hadn't been out together in quite a while.

His mood took a nose dive when he reached the end of his driveway and saw Luce on the deck, cigarette in one hand, bottle of beer in the other.

Without thinking twice, Will knew the best part of his day was behind him.

\*\*\*

"So, how's Carol doing?" Smoke drifted from Luce's mouth as she spoke.

"Sore, stubborn, brave, stupid; take your pick." Will glanced at the beer in her hand.

She tilted her head and pursed her lips. "I know, it's early, but it's been that kind of day. Want me to get you one?"

Will shook his head. "I'll bring us both one soon as I wash up." He held up his hand, fingers splayed. "Five minutes."

He ruffled her hair as he went past.

"Okey dokey."

Her sing-song answer told him the beer wasn't her first. And smoking again? Inside, he turned on the taps and soaped his hands, his mother's words coming back to him. "Help her if you can, Will. She's had a hard life, son. You understand." He did understand. None of the beatings he took from Ray – not when Ray broke his nose and cracked his ribs, or the time he kicked him in the head hard enough to knock him out –compared to the hell Luce found herself in after her parents died. He sympathized. He really did, but at times he wanted to grab her by the shoulders and shake common sense into her. She wasn't the tough little cynic she pretended, but her impulsive nature had a way of landing her in trouble.

He dried his hands, changed into a clean tee shirt and khakis, and grabbed two beers from the fridge.

\*\*\*

Luce chugged the rest of her beer the minute Will entered the house. She shook a fresh cigarette from its pack, lighting it from the remains of the last. She dragged the smoke in deep, held it as long as she could, and exhaled. Smoke streamed from her mouth and hung in the air like a distant memory.

How she missed Rose. Losing her had been almost as bad as losing her parents in that stupid car accident. They'd met by chance at the library where Luce took her sons for story hour every week. Rose worked there and she read the stories. Soon they began talking. A few weeks later, Rose invited them to dinner. Luce accepted. Rose lived in an apartment in an older section of Portland. Inside, a series of doors stretched down a long hallway, each a dreary brown but for Rose's, painted a periwinkle blue; a wreath of seashells and sea grass fixed at its center. Walking through that door for the first time and seeing Rose's smile of welcome, was like coming home again after a long absence. For a moment, the strength of that feeling overwhelmed her. She had thrust the supermarket cone of pink carnations and purple iris into Rose's hands, too tongue-tied to speak. Rose had exclaimed over the supermarket flowers as though she'd never been given flowers before.

Spaghetti with meatballs. Wonderful, crunchy bread. A checkered tablecloth with a candle dripping colored wax down the sides of a wine bottle. Luce believed no restaurant in town, no matter how fancy, could compare to the welcoming warmth of Rose's little kitchen with its gingham curtains, spice bottles in wooden racks, and small pots of herbs on the windowsill.

Dinners became a weekly affair. Soon, she and Rose shared stories of their pasts. She met Rose's son, Will, who had done his best – more than his best – to help her back on her feet after her fiasco with pain pills. She owed him big-time, but she was drying up here, dying of boredom and missing her children. If she stayed much longer, she knew she might fall back into the pointless affair with Ben just to pass the time.

"Damn!" Luce flung her cigarette into the yard and examined her finger. A blister was forming where the tip had burned down and into her skin. She shook her head in disgust. Christ! I can't even smoke a cigarette without screwing up.

Behind her, the screen door opened then closed. Will, holding two frosty bottles, took a seat beside her.

"Here you go."

"Thanks." Luce took one, running her burned finger up and down the icy neck.

Will took a long swallow, set his bottle down, and took Luce's hand. "Okay," he said, what's going on."

# 32

**D**amn it, Will's right. I do feel worse today, like I've been run over by a truck.

Will said nothing when she hobbled out to meet him. He didn't have to. His expression said it all.

By mid-morning, an exasperated Sarah led her to a client's picnic table. "Sit, and don't you dare move, or I will shoot you and end your misery for good!"

Carol discovered then that laughing hurt.

Sarah shook her finger. "Don't laugh. I may look soft but I'm one mean mother when crossed."

A statement that caused Carol even greater pain.

"One more day," Will said, when he delivered her back home. "You do know you can stay home tomorrow, right?"

"Yes, I do," she replied, "but I won't. See you tomorrow morning, Will."

She waited until he was out of sight before she limped to the house. Inside, she poured a tall glass of iced tea before she noticed the glowing red eye on the answering machine.

She put in her code and waited.

"Carol, Dave Linfield here. I believe I've struck pay dirt. Give me a call when you get this."

She dialed his number.

"What did I tell you?" His excitement pulsed through the line. "You aren't the only woman Malone messed with. I contacted the community college where he taught before he showed up in Fairfield. He left before his contract ended. Personnel refused to give me anything except his dates of employment, but when I told the clerk I was investigating an assault charge I swear I could *feel* her attitude change. She asked for my phone number and promised to call me back. Hold on a sec."

Static interrupted, a garbled voice requested a license check.

"Sorry for the interruption," he said, back on again. "I'm manning the radio today. Anyhow, within an hour I got a call from a Krystal Lieuallen. She was luckier than you, Carol. She got off with a broken wrist. She was too embarrassed – or scared – to press charges, but she did tell a co-worker. He reported the incident to the college president. Malone left right after that."

"So this woman will testify?"

"She'll sign a deposition, but she won't appear. She's married now, expecting her first child. She won't go anywhere near Tom Malone, says she still has nightmares about him."

\*\*\*

Thursday, Carol reveled in a perfect morning as she waited outside. Rose petal clouds skimmed a robin's egg sky. Nest-building mud swallows swooped around the house eaves, and the creek sang through the trees. The day ahead stretched like a lover's promise and made her glad to be alive.

"You look better," Will said, when she climbed into his pickup.

"Thanks, I feel better." And she did. She had slept the night through, waking with barely a twinge. Her bruises were fading to a sulfurous yellow and her lips no longer looked like silicone injections gone bad. "I had some good news from Dave, too."

"What kind of news?"

"Looks like Tom stalked another woman before me. She's giving a deposition for use at his trial."

"So this time he won't get away with it."

"Nope, hopefully not." Carol leaned her head against Lady, running her hand up and down her back. Lady reciprocated with a long, wet lick to the side of her face.

Ben was sweeping the store porch when they drove by. Will tooted the horn and got a wave of the broom in response.

"I haven't seen Ben since your barbecue."

"Me neither," Will replied. "I meant to call him yesterday but wound up having a long talk with Luce instead."

"About what, if I'm not too nosy?"

"Looks like I'm taking her to Portland this weekend. Otherwise, she tells me she'll hit the highway with her thumb out."

"She'd hitchhike? You're kidding."

"No, I'm not. She's done it before." He shook his head. "Luce thinks she can handle herself in spite of how many times she's failed."

"Will, you can't blame her for missing the life she's used to."

"I don't," he said. "But things won't be easy for her in Portland, and if she falls in with the wrong people again…" His voice drifted off. He downshifted and slowed, turning into a cul-de-sac near the river. He left the engine idling, set the hand brake, and turned to face her.

"Luce was twelve when her parents died in a car wreck," Will said. "Her only living relative was an aunt in Salem, a religious fanatic. Luce ran away after two months. Her aunt didn't bother to report her missing."

"You mean she washed her hands of a twelve-year-old child?"

"Yep. But Luce lucked out. She made it to Portland and found a shelter for runaways – she had a bed to sleep in, three meals a day, and classes to keep her from falling behind in school. Things might have worked for her except for the frat brat who tutored at the shelter. He singled her out, made her feel special. She was too naïve to recognize a snow job."

"She had a crush on him; that's not unusual."

"Yes, she had a crush on him. So when he invited her to his frat party and told her to keep it secret, she did. After lights out, she went out a window to meet him. He took her to a party, all right. He slipped a little something into her punch, waited until she passed out, and proceeded to share her with a few of his so-called brothers."

"Oh, God."

"God wasn't around," Will said bitterly. "At least not all of those boys were jerks. One called the cops because he couldn't stop what was happening. They arrived to find Luce unconscious. The boys responsible scattered to the four winds. Luce went to the hospital. While she was recovering, she learned she'd been evicted from the shelter for breaking the rules and would be sent to a juvenile facility after her discharge. She sneaked out that evening. You can imagine what she did to survive."

Will lapsed into silence. Carol thought of herself at that age, loved and supported by her parents and uncle. She couldn't imagine what Luce must have gone through, having no one and no place to go.

"No one else knows, Carol, not even Rick and Lorrie, but Luce has two sons. That's the real reason she's eager to return to Portland."

"What?"

"Yeah. They're in foster care. Luce got involved with the wrong man. She broke it off, but he beat her to a pulp before he took off. She had to be hospitalized."

Carol closed her eyes. She and Luce had more in common than she realized.

Will released the handbrake, shifted into first gear, and coasted back onto the highway, still talking. "She had no insurance, no money, and no one to look after her kids. A social worker suggested foster care until Luce got back on her feet."

They drove by a group of children waiting for the school bus. They waved. Carol waved back.

"Luce got hooked on her pain medication," Will continued. "When she left the hospital she forged a prescription. The pharmacist called the police. Given her history, the judge at her hearing wasn't inclined toward leniency."

"What history?"

"Arrests for prostitution and check kiting. I talked with the judge and explained what she'd been through. He gave her probation rather than jail time, if she agreed to stay in Winter with me until the time was up."

"I'm guessing her time isn't up but she intends to leave anyway?"

Will nodded his head.

"And you're caught in the middle," Carol said. "Do you threaten her with notifying the Court, or do you remain silent and hope she keeps a low profile until her probation is over?

"Exactly." Will sighed. "Luce is going whether I take her or not. I'd rather see that she gets to Portland in one piece and give her enough money for rent and food until she starts drawing a paycheck. She claims she's getting her old job back at the bar. I want to confirm that, too."

"I'm sorry, Will. Tell me how I can help."

Will's hand dropped to Lady's head in his lap. "Would you mind keeping Lady until I get back?"

# 33

Luce took a final look around at the room that had been hers the last few months. Pale terra cotta walls that took the light and gave it back, windows that framed a view of miniature pine and river rock. As soon as Will left for work, she'd stripped the bed and washed the sheets. While they dried, she packed, taking only what clothes she needed along with framed photo of her sons she'd kept under her pillow. She didn't think Will would mind her taking one of his backpacks. It wasn't as if they'd never see each other again.

Now, dressed in a flowered skirt – short but not too short – and a pale yellow tank top that highlighted her honey-gold skin, she studied the effect in the dresser mirror. Satisfied, she cocked a hip and flashed what her old boss used to call a come hither smile. With luck, she'd be in Portland by nightfall. Someone on the way to Pendleton would stop for her. Once she reached the truck stop at Mission, catching a ride to Portland should be a snap. Years of hitching rides had taught her that most truckers were decent guys, and she was savvy enough to pick the right ones. Still, she couldn't rid herself of a nagging sense of guilt. Damn Will. He knew she hated good-byes. Yet he'd made her promise not to take off on her own, to wait until he was free so he could drive her. She agreed, only to end the discussion. What other choice did she have? Dear Will. He thought Portland held temptation. He didn't know she'd embraced it here by sleeping with Ben. Heck, he knew she could take care of herself. Well, most of the time, anyway. It wasn't as if she hadn't planned ahead: a girlfriend to stay with until she earned enough for her own apartment, and a job at the bar where she used to work. All she had to do was keep her head down. When her probation ended, she and the boys would be a family again.

Luce fingered an earring with a pang of guilt. She hadn't taken her dream catchers off since the day Will gave them to her. Rose and Will. They had been so good to her and the boys.

She took a deep breath, picked up the backpack, and walked from the room.

An ancient pickup splotched with rust and belching oily smoke stopped for her less than fifty feet past Will's driveway. Its driver, a skinny guy with a scraggly goatee, bloodshot eyes and a nervous tic imitating a smile, leaned over and pushed open the passenger door.

"Goin' to town?"

Damn! One of the dope camp creeps. Luce looked him over, figured she could take him one-handed if he tried anything, and nodded.

No handle on the inside of the door. What the hell. The window was down. She could open the door from outside if necessary.

She shivered with excitement in spite of the driver's sour odor and her mode of transportation. She was on her way!

They hadn't gone more than two miles before she saw Jackson Henry walking toward them on the opposite side of the road. He was one of her favorite people and she would miss him. He'd been so sweet, dancing with her the night of the party.

Luce felt her resolve weakening. Sure, she wanted to leave, but like this? Throwing the kindness of these people back in their faces? Taking off without so much as a thank you?

Maybe it's time you grew up, Lucinda.

"Stop!" she demanded, surprising herself as much as the driver.

He didn't seem to hear, or if he did, ignored her.

"I said stop!" She grabbed the steering wheel and wrenched it to one side.

He hit the brakes and the pickup wobbled off the road.

"What the hell!"

"Thanks," Luce said, "but I've changed my mind. I don't need a ride after all."

The dirt-grained hand that grasped her forearm was surprisingly strong. "Sure about that, sugar?" he muttered through cracked lips.

She tried to pull her arm away. His grip tightened.

"Let me go, you idiot..."

The idiot gave a strangled cry and began to flail his arms, hands flopping. His knees came up and rammed against the bottom of the steering wheel and his feet hammered against the floor. His face, red at first, turned a dangerous shade of blue. Luce watched in disbelief as he began to levitate until his head reached the roof of the cab. Then she realized a huge hand held him by the neck.

Jackson.

She scrabbled outside the window for the door handle, found it. Pushed the door open and jumped down to the pavement.

"Jackson," she yelled, "Stop. Let him go."

This Jackson scared her. Gone the shy, gentle man she thought she knew, in his place the avenging angel her crazy aunt used to threaten her with: the one who wreaked vengeance on sinners, especially little girls who took less than an hour at their bedtime prayers, or who laughed when they shouldn't, or liked to listen to music only the damned enjoyed.

Her scream broke his hold. He let go and his victim dropped back onto the seat, a scarecrow robbed of straw. His head lolled back. Raw, sucking gasps came from his throat as his mouth worked for air. His color gradually shaded from blue to puce. He tried to restart the engine, but his shaking hand couldn't manage the key. Jackson reached in and turned it for him. The engine coughed, caught, and backfired. Leaning over the steering wheel, barely able to hold his head up, the man drove off, black smoke trailing from the bent tailpipe as the pickup shuddered from side to side until it disappeared.

"Thanks, Big J," Luce said, rubbing the imprint of fingers from her arm. "I think I could have taken him, but your way was quicker." She laughed. "The look on his face when you –"

"What did you think you were doing?" Jackson's voice crackled with anger.

"Hitching a ride into town," she said, suddenly sober. "But I changed my mind."

"Hitching?" A single word so filled with contempt that Luce flinched.

"I know. Dumb idea."

"Worse than dumb." He looked at her, then up and down the road. "My place is close. Come on. I'll get my car and drive you back to Will's."

# 34

The boy comes of age, goes out into the world. He works his way through college, gets a job and after years of searching, finds his mother.

She's living with someone. Surprise, surprise. A grizzle-faced, droopy-eyed loser with a mean curl to his mouth, a carbon copy of all the men she paraded through their childhood.

No longer beautiful, his mother is a fat, drunken slob who bursts into sloppy tears the moment she opens the pockmarked door and sees him standing in the vile-smelling hallway. She pulls him inside the two-room apartment dim as a church, a place in perpetual twilight no matter the time or weather. Wallpaper stained and peeling, windows painted shut, torn brown shades on rickety rollers. She sits him down in an ancient easy chair marked with years of cigarette burns, takes a seat in a sagging armchair across from him, and reaches for a bottle on the scarred table between them. She takes a drink before offering the bottle: cheap blackberry wine. Mad Dog. He shakes his head. All he wants to know is what became of Alec. She stares at him through bleary eyes, wipes a snail trail of snot above her mouth and takes a long pull on the bottle before answering. "Gone," she says, "Alec's gone." Her mouth twists. Saliva sprays from her lips when she adds, "Your fault, you little shit. You were supposed to watch him." The exact same words she snarled before two policemen led her away. Her eyes roll, then close. Her head lolls forward. Hoarse snores follow. Her breath adds to the stench of the already befouled air. He sits staring at this – this thing that was his mother, and in a moment of supreme clarity, knows what he must do. Glancing toward the kitchenette, he sees her boyfriend cracking eggs into a smoking skillet; his back turned. The man reaches across the table and covers his mother's nose and mouth with the palm of his hand. Her struggle is brief, no more than a hiccup, but he is startled when her eyes, so like Alec's, so like his own, snap open and fix on his. Is it gratitude he sees in them? When it's done, he rises from his chair. His erection is huge, unexpected.

His mother's boyfriend still mumbles over the frying pan, oblivious to what took place under his nose. The man feels hollow, light as a paper husk, like the windfall apples he once came across scattered beneath a tree. They seemed ordinary, lying there; rosy-skinned, a few worm holes pocking their skin, but when he bent to pick one up, it was like holding a ball of air. Through a rent in the skin he saw cannibalized flesh. Five or six nasty looking wasps still crawled inside. Disgusted, he had dropped the apple to the ground and crushed it beneath his foot.

Something far more dangerous than wasps crawls inside him now.

When he leaves, the boyfriend is hunched over his burned eggs, and does not look up.

# 35

Will arrived home looking forward to finally hitting the river. He left Lady waiting outside when he went in to change, but the minute he walked through the door he knew something was wrong. Silence. Luce always had a radio or CD going. She couldn't bear the quiet. With a sickening feeling he checked her room. The stripped bed and empty surface of the dresser confirmed his fear. He checked the closet. Empty. In spite of their talk and her promise, she'd taken off. He pounded the wall with his fist. Dammit! But his anger was at himself, not her. He should have known this would happen. When had Luce ever listened to reason? He should have left Gerry in charge at work and driven her to Portland right away instead of asking her to wait.

He left the room, shutting the door behind him. Fishing forgotten, he snagged a beer from the fridge and popped the cap. That's when he noticed her house key on the table. He drained half the beer in a single swallow and picked up the phone. He might be able to reach her on her cell. Whether or not she'd answer, though... He dialed, heard a few bars of Aretha Franklin singing, *Think*. Luce's voice: "You've found me. Leave a message."

He tried Carol next. "She's gone," he blurted, when she answered.

"But I thought –"

"She told me what I wanted to hear then waited for me to leave so she could get away without an argument. I tried calling her cell phone. She isn't picking up."

"She'll call, won't she, once she reaches Portland?"

"I hope so, but if I know Luce, she'll wait until she thinks I've calmed down."

"So, will you still drive down this weekend anyway, to check on her?"

"I don't know. I'm so damn mad right now, I can't think."

"I'm so sorry, Will."

"Yeah, me too. I'll let you know if I have any news." He hung up, too pissed off to bother with goodbye.

\*\*\*

This isn't happening.

Luce turned her head from side to side, taking in the dim and sparsely furnished room. Bedside table, closet door, the top of an old steamer trunk showing above the end of the bed. Two windows, both shut, covered by ordinary brown shades. A small tear in one bled drops of bright light. Stuff taped to the walls that she couldn't make out

Duct tape sealed her lips, and bound her hands together behind her back. Her fingers were growing numb beneath her body weight and she squirmed, trying to ease the pressure. Beneath her, the plastic sheet crinkled.

A sob threatened to choke her.

Beyond the closed door came ordinary, everyday sounds: the clink of silverware, water flowing through pipes, a cupboard door, opening and closing.

Why?

Hours passed. Shadows crept up the walls and met on the ceiling. The tiny trickle of light from the torn blind disappeared.

I need to pee.

A key scraped the lock. The door swung open, bringing a draft of cold air. Her naked flesh puckered, but not from the cold. Her heart drummed in her ears. She strained her eyes to pierce the dark, to see his face. Maybe then she might understand.

The mattress sagged. She heard him breathing. Cool fingers traced the planes of her face, the line of her throat. His hand encircled her neck, squeezed gently, and moved on.

Her breath caught when the hand found her breast. She twisted, but he pinched her nostrils together with his free hand until she surrendered and lay still.

His mouth replaced his hand, teeth teasing the nipple – uncomfortable, but not painful. Luce fought panic. She had suffered worse. If she used her head, if she played along, she might yet walk away from this.

The hand continued its journey, sliding over her ribs, the inward curve of her waist, the fullness of her hip. It stopped, and for a breathless moment, she hoped he was done.

He wasn't.

Crablike, the hand scuttled between her thighs. Hot tears scalded her cheeks. His breath quickened as his fingers explored. Moaning with shame, she lost control of her bladder. Wetness surged between her legs, over his hand.

He hurt her then.

# 36

After his call to Carol, Will paced, unable to concentrate. Damn Luce. Another couple of months and she could have returned to Portland, reclaimed her sons, and started a new life. Eight lousy weeks, yet she couldn't wait.

Lady's sharp bark reminded him he'd left her outside. He'd join her, walk off this mood. By the time they reached the river, his mood should improve. When they got back, he'd try calling Luce again.

He and Lady cut across the yard and entered the meadow, Lady dancing with excitement all the way. They were nearing the tree line when he spotted Jackson. Deep in thought, the big man remained unaware of them until Lady barked. His head came up. He waved, and quickened his steps to meet them.

"Luce make it home okay?"

"You saw her?"

"Yes," Jackson said. "This morning. She was trying to extricate herself from a pickup." He frowned, turning his forehead into a map of lines. "Belonged to one of those camp bums. The driver didn't want to let her out." A slow smile erased the lines. "I changed his mind. I offered to get my car and drive Luce home Will, but she refused. Said she had some thinking to do and walking would help her sort things out."

Will's heart sank. Leave it to Luce. The minute Jackson turned his back she would have stuck her thumb out again, hoping for a more trustworthy ride.

"She's gone, Jackson."

"What?"

"She never came home."

"I sh-should have insisted on taking her. I'm sorry, Will."

"Don't be. Luce does what Luce wants. She wanted to go to Portland. I told her I'd take her this weekend but she wouldn't wait. Hell, by now she's probably there. Hopefully, she'll call me this evening."

"You'll let me know?" Jackson looked so woebegone Will wanted to pat him on the shoulder, say, 'there, there.' He resisted the impulse and watched Jackson shamble away, shoulders slumped.

He and Lady took off again, picking up their pace until they broke through the trees to the river. While Lady chased minnows in the shallows, Will sat on a downed log watching the Umatilla flow past. Calmer now, he realized he had to let Luce choose her own path. He wouldn't give her hell when she called. He would tell her to stay in touch, to let him know if she needed anything. Tomorrow was her day to call her boys' foster parents. She never missed a Friday call. If he didn't hear from her by Sunday, he could call them, but what reason could he give without admitting Luce had broken probation and returned to Portland? No, all he could do was wait, and hope she had the good sense to contact him.

# 37

Carol fastened her seat belt. She didn't need to ask Will if he'd heard from Luce. The answer lay in the set of his jaw and his grip on the steering wheel. She'd checked with him Saturday but his terse, "nothing yet," had kept her from bothering him again.

"I made a few calls yesterday evening," he said, once they were on their way. "I called her friend, Penny, the gal she was supposed to stay with until she got back on her feet. Penny hasn't heard from her." His fingers opened and closed on the steering wheel. "She didn't seem worried. In fact, she sounded seriously stoned." He took his eyes from the road for an instant and glanced at her. "I tried the bar where she was supposed to have a job. Same story. I saved the foster home for last. Luce never called Friday. That's what bothers me the most. She always calls on Friday. Always."

"Why don't you talk to Dave? File a missing person report."

"I'm going to see him after I drop you at Wilma's."

"Good." After a few miles of strained silence, Carol thought of a safe topic. "I saw Ben at the river yesterday afternoon. Talk about a contented man."

"Fishing?"

"Yes." Seeing Ben in his element had put him in a whole new light. Used to his ever-present smile and outrageous jokes, Carol had barely recognized the serene man in hip waders and fishing vest, thigh-deep in a quiet pool shaded by cottonwoods. She had watched, unobserved, as he cast his line, teasing the water's dappled surface with the fly again and again before letting it come to rest. It was like a moment out of time, river and man mystically joined by that single, lucent strand of fishing line.

\*\*\*

Filing a report proved as difficult as Will feared.

Deputy Baldwin sat behind the counter.

"Dave here?"

"Dave has the day off."

"How about Sheriff McReady?"

"Attending a conference in Madras on rural crime." Baldwin smiled. "You're stuck with me."

Will nodded, hoping his disappointment didn't show. Baldwin certainly seemed efficient the day he picked up Malone, but he looked so damn young.

The deputy left his desk and approached the counter, serious now. "What can I do for you, Will?"

"Help me with a missing persons report."

Baldwin nodded, walked to a file cabinet, opened a drawer and removed a form. He placed it between them. "Talk to me."

Baldwin remained silent while Will laid out his concerns. When he finished, the deputy scratched the side of his nose. "Okay, let's consider what we know." One finger shot up. "By your own admission, Luce has done this kind of thing before." A second finger joined the first. "Also, by your own admission, she is impulsive." When Baldwin's third finger took a place beside the other two, Will had a sudden vision of the young deputy reciting the Boy Scout pledge. He gripped the edge of the counter to keep from slapping the hand down.

Baldwin must have read his mind because the hand dropped below the counter, out of sight. He wasn't finished talking, however. "Have you considered she found a ride at the truck stop and let some trucker talk her into going cross country with him? Is she that impulsive?"

Will took an impatient breath, let it out. "Years ago? Maybe. Not now."

"Okay." Baldwin thrummed his fingers on the counter for a moment, thinking. "What are the chances the girlfriend – Penny, you said – is lying to you?"

"She could be," Will said, "but why would Luce's old boss?" He leaned forward until his face was inches from Baldwin's. "Why am I getting the impression you don't want to act on this? The foster parents have no reason to lie. Luce did not contact them."

Will's growing irritation left Baldwin unfazed. "Give me a couple of days. I'll get her description out, make a couple of calls, ask the Portland police to check her old haunts. I'm just afraid we won't learn much. Chances are she'll contact you when she's ready." His hands went to the knot on his tie, tightening it. "I can tell you, no reports of death or injury to anyone fitting her description have been posted. That's good news, at least."

"Thanks. I'll check in with you tomorrow."

"Sure. And Will? Have a little faith. She's only been gone since Thursday."

Will left feeling short on faith. Once Baldwin ran Luce's name through the system and learned of her previous record, he'd be even more convinced she was okay, lying low so she couldn't be picked up for violating her probation. Will wanted to believe that too, but his gut told him otherwise.

# 38

The past strikes without warning, rising like a Golem from the sad dust of memory. The man sees a silent little boy of five with dazed eyes. When this happens, his insides drop away. He tries to reach across the years to embrace the child but cannot breach the invisible barrier that separates them, cannot gather that lost child in his arms to beg his forgiveness. He stands helpless, unable to remedy what can never be made right, while that night replays over and over in his head like a loop of cracked celluloid, forcing him to relive again the dull thud of a small head against a wall, his mother's screams mixing with the wail of sirens, revolving lights on police cars and ambulance drenching the faces of the curious with a color like blood.

His fault. She told him, she warned him, but he didn't obey. The man mourns for the child lying limp in the arms of the screaming woman. He sees himself, a child of ten, helpless, watching a stretcher roll out the front door, the small body on it so pale, the eyes open and staring. That child is... No! Even now he cannot say that word. His head threatens to explode. His rage builds and his nails cut into his palms, leaving crescent shapes on his flesh for days. She did it. She brought evil into their home and left him with nothing.

He unlocks the bedroom door and pushes it open. The air that meets him is rich with bruised flesh and bodily fluids. Heat surges through his groin. If only he could delay the inevitable, punish her a few more days, but it's too dangerous. Besides, she's nearly gone as it is. He fingers his new talisman. The silver is slick, warm to the touch, the small turquoise stones only slightly rough. "I missed you, Luce," he whispers, stepping into the room, locking the door behind him.

\*\*\*

Luce drifts in and out of consciousness. She feels the sun through the lowered blinds and forces her lids open to stare at the ceiling. She won't look down. She cannot bear the battleground her body has become.

God, the smell. How can he stand the smell?

Her eyes close. Blood pulses through her ears. Wait. Not blood. Waves. Waves hissing and whispering on the shore. She's at the beach with Mom and Dad. She's shivering because the beach is cold this time of year. Mom says they can only afford the beach when rates are cheaper, but cold doesn't matter when you're having fun. Luce sucks in a lungful of iodine-tainted air and dreams the Pacific is flowing up onto the sand, white froth dancing, searching every nook and cranny, feeling its way toward her. She's eight and Mommy holds her hand while waves roll over their feet. The froth bubbles around their ankles. White mice, her mother calls it. White mice body surfing on our feet. Luce giggles. Mommy leads her into deeper water. It's up to her waist now, warm, and spangled with sun. "Relax, my Lucy-Lou, lie back," Mommy whispers. "Let the water hold you." She's afraid at first, but Mommy supports her and when her hands drop away, Luce discovers that the water does hold her, and she has nothing to be afraid of, nothing at all.

# 39

"You can't blame Baldwin, Will," Carol said that afternoon. "You expected as much from Dave."

"Yeah, I know. All the same, I'm calling Dave later. I don't want Luce pushed to a back burner because of her record." His mouth settled into a grim line.

Carol wished she could erase the tiredness from his face, hated she had so little help to offer. She'd talked with Lorrie a couple of times, hoping for advice, but though she was sympathetic, she was also pragmatic.

"Will knew what he was getting into when he brought Luce here," she'd said. "He's done his best, but she's a grown woman. He can't live her life for her."

"Carol?"

"I'm sorry. Guess I was woolgathering."

"I asked if you were up for a drive later this evening. Remember stargazing on Thornhollow grade?

She smiled. "I remember, but what if Luce calls?"

"My cell works fine up there."

\*\*\*

At home, Carol threw a load of clothes in the washing machine and emptied the dishwasher. She had time to weed the vegetable garden but wanted to run to the store first, buy a little surprise for Will. She grabbed her keys and headed for the car.

When she reached the store, the Murphy family's dust-covered Ford Escort sat in the parking lot.

She found them inside. Susan, a fragile, fair-skinned and fair-haired woman, was dressed in crisp white slacks and yellow tee, and cradled a small bundle in her arms, her husband, Connor, all six feet of him, beside her. Red hair flamed from under his dark blue ball cap. A Seattle Mariners shirt fell outside his well-worn jeans. They appeared much too young to be parents of three. Their two older children, Cassie and Colin, pressed against the counter, eyes fixed on Ben, who held a glass jar filled with red and black licorice whips.

"Hi, Carol," he called when she came in. "Be with you in a sec, soon as these scallywags make up their minds."

"Scallywags? What's a scallywags?" piped five-year old Cassie.

Ben laughed. "Whatever you want it to be, sweetheart." He held the jar closer. "So, red or black?"

A pudgy finger found its way to Cassie's lips. Choosing was hard.

Big brother Colin had no such dilemma. "Black, please."

Ben unscrewed the lid. "Tell you what, kids. Why not take one of each?"

"I'm sorry, Susan," Carol said, "but I've forgotten the new baby's name."

"It's Craig," Connor said. "Take a look. He's fast asleep." He pulled aside a corner of green blanket.

Carol reached out and lightly stroked wisps of strawberry blonde hair. "He's beautiful. Connor, are all your children's names going to start with C?"

Connor laughed. "I think we're through with C's for the time being." He glanced at his wife, one side of his mouth curving upward. "Aren't we, honey?"

"We better be," she answered, then winked.

Ben whooped with laughter.

Carol went to the freezer and chose two ice cream bars. When she stepped up to the counter to pay, Connor and Ben had their heads together. Carol heard one word – "hatch."

Susan shrugged, mouthed, "Fish talk."

"Come on, Connor," Susan said. "We need to get home. Craig's going to want his dinner soon."

"I'll catch you later, Ben," Connor said. "Maybe the boss lady will let me off duty one night so we can go fishing. Good bye Carol," he said, tipping his cap. "Nice seeing you again."

Ben's eyes followed them out the door. "It's too darn quiet here after they've left."

Carol nodded. "I know what you mean. They're a beautiful family." She placed her money on the counter. "You have a real knack with kids, Ben. Cassie and Colin adore you. And those bubble kits you brought for the kids the night of the party? *That* was inspired."

Ben smiled. "I think Joe Wright had more fun than the kids." His eyes brightened. "I love kids. The smallest things excite them."

Carol thought it a shame Ben had no family of his own but didn't say so. She knew he'd been married a long time ago but for whatever reason, it hadn't lasted.

"You're miles away, Carol. What are you thinking?"

She shook her head. "Reliving a memory, I guess. That's why the ice cream bars."

Ben's eyebrows shot up. "Tell me."

"Uncle James used to take us kids to Thornhollow Grade to study the stars. In the summer he'd pack these in a cooler for us. In the winter it was Twinkies and hot chocolate in a thermos."

Was she mistaken, or did she see a fleeting sadness in those blue eyes?

"Every kid should have an Uncle James," Ben said. "You were lucky."

Carol nodded and reached for the bag Ben pushed across the counter. "Will and I are going up there tonight. Now I'd better get these home to the freezer."

"No word on Luce, yet, I guess," he said before she could move.

"No, Ben. Afraid not. Will filed a missing person report this morning but the deputy who took it wasn't very encouraging."

"I've wracked my brain since I heard, trying to remember who passed the store that day on their way into Pendleton." He pushed his hands into his pockets. "Trouble is, it was a quiet day and I spent the better part of it in back, tying flies."

He came from behind the counter and walked Carol to the door. Opening it he said, "Luce is a tough cookie. She'll turn up."

Would he sound so sure if he knew about Luce's sons, her failure to call their foster parents Friday? "I hope you're right, Ben," Carol said. "I'll see you later."

*** 

Ben watched Carol drive away. Odd look on her face when he assured her Luce would turn up. Luce. He felt bad for Will, he really did. Word of her departure had traveled through the canyon, as news here always did. Reactions varied. Cora Newsome, of course, lost no time in expressing her feelings. "Water seeks its own level," she had snapped.

Whatever in hell that meant.

He ran a hand over his face, finding a patch of stubble his razor missed. A faint smear of blood showed on his hand. Damn razor cut from yesterday still hadn't healed.

"What the hell," he muttered and crossed the floor to flip the sign from Open to Closed. No reason to stay indoors on a day like this. An hour or two at the river had much more appeal.

# 40

Will turned off the engine.

In the west, a crimson sun hovered on the horizon. Bars of hot pink, magenta and gold streaked the sky. To the south the mountains looked close enough to touch, the air was that clear. Below then, the canyon floor resembled a tapestry woven of many colors shot through with the glistening threads of creeks and river.

"You have no idea," Will said, staring out the windshield, "how much those outings with your uncle meant to me." He rested his arm on the back of the seat. "He gave me my first fishing rod. Did you know that?"

Carol felt the warmth of his fingers against the nape of her neck. "No, but I'm not surprised."

"It was the summer before I met you. He saw me at the creek one day, trying to fish with a bent pole Mom had found at a yard sale. Cost a whole quarter. Next day he showed up with a little fly fishing rod, said it was an old one he had lying around and didn't need any more." Will smiled at the memory. "He said he'd teach me to cast, and gave me a little aluminum box with two flies he'd tied himself." His smile disappeared. "Ray broke the pole in half a few months later. My punishment for not getting a beer to him fast enough."

Ray. Carol wanted no mention of him to mar her memories of this place. "Come on, let's get outside." She depressed the door handle and slid from the seat, taking her ice pack with her.

They leaned against the front bumper, shoulder to shoulder, absorbed in the spectacular view. Lady ran from one spot to another, nose to the ground, lost in scent heaven. Deer and coyotes foraged. Badgers, rabbits, and other small creatures made their homes here, providing a treasure trove of rich and intriguing smells.

The sun began to slip beneath the horizon, a globe dipped in fire. Carol took a deep, contented breath, inhaling the wild sage that rode on a southerly breeze, and reached into her pack.

Will's face lit up when he saw what she held. "You remembered!" He accepted an ice cream bar from her, opened the wrapper and took a bite. "I haven't had one of these in years."

The sun disappeared as they ate. A sprinkling of stars appeared over the mountains.

When Will finished, he folded his wrapper and tucked it into his vest pocket. He reached for Carol's hand. "Remember James' story about the Pleiades?"

"You mean the Ute Indian legend?" With her eyes on the stars, she recited the tale from memory. "Within the tribe, there were a group of children who loved to dance. Their parents warned them against dancing everyday, but they didn't listen. One evening they danced too long and became so lightheaded they floated into the sky. Their parents saw what was happening and called out to them but they were too late."

Carol squeezed his hand. "Remember the rest?"

"One child turned into a meteor, the others rose higher and higher until they turned into stars." He smiled. "James taught us without our realizing."

"There's more, Will. Remember Singing Boy? By the time he reached his new home in the sky, he could scarcely be seen." Her voice grew soft. "I never liked that part. It made me sad to think of that little boy alone, without parents or friends."

\*\*\*

That night Carol dreamed. In that dream she woke to the smell of coffee and cigarette smoke coming from downstairs. She threw on a robe and hurried down, aware that her feet never touched the risers.

James sat in his rocker, pen and sketchbook balanced on his lap, a small lamp on a side table throwing a pool of light on his lap and hands. Steam rose from a chipped mug. Smoke from the hand-rolled cigarette held spiraled up and disappeared into the shadows overhead. With a cry, she floated across the distance between them, leaned down and hugged him. "I missed you so much, Uncle."

James chuckled. "I missed you too, lightning bug."

Before she could say more, the scene dissolved. She came to in the dark, leaning over an empty rocker. So vivid had been her dream, she still smelled coffee and smoke, remembered the worn softness of his flannel shirt, the sandpaper roughness of her uncle's cheek when they hugged. Logic claimed her evening with Will, talking of her uncle, brought the dream. But as she climbed the stairs back to bed, Carol believed in more. Uncle James had found a way to let her know he loved her still.

\*\*\*

Jackson fiddled with his radio. Static on every station. Disgusted, he gave up, switched it off, and ran a meaty finger over his CDs, bypassing Brahms and Beethoven for *Opera's Greatest Moments*. He rearranged the peacock feathers in the vase next to the player before falling into his oversized Lazy Boy.

In spite of the music, his mind refused to settle.

Luce. If only she had accepted his offer to drive her home.

She had been good to him, never making fun of his size, or the bashful stammer that embarrassment brought. 'Big man,' she might have called him, but with affection, not contempt. She'd made him feel normal, not some freak of nature.

Baby Huey, Godzilla, King Kong, names he'd been called since early childhood. By the time he reached twelve, he stood six feet four inches, and the entire world seemed to mock him. Adults expected him to act like an adult because of his size. Kids his age found him freakish. And girls? They ran from him.

The night they danced together had been one of the happiest he'd known. She'd been so light in his arms, and for a few magical moments her closed eyes and sweet, trusting smile had turned him from ugly frog into a prince, making up for the miserable years in high school when every girl he approached for a dance faded into the crowd to avoid him.

Pain shot through his temples. He gripped his head between his hands and squeezed, trying to contain his thoughts. But one memory returned to haunt him. The music, he told himself, concentrate on the music, on Anna Moffo's gorgeous voice. But like a rogue wave, the past swept over him, the undertow dragging him back.

*Summer. He's sixteen, taking the long way home in hopes he might catch a glimpse of Sharon Lenihan, the girl of his dreams. For once, luck is with him because as he approaches her house, she flounces from her back door wearing an electric blue bikini. A beach towel is draped over one arm.*

*She spots him and, miracle of miracles, waves before she spreads the towel on the grass and arranges herself over it.*

*He should keep walking, but can't take his eyes from her long, blonde hair, her smooth, tanned skin. At that moment, a terrible truth seizes him. He will always be on the outside looking in, an oversized curiosity denied what so many other take for granted.*

*His throat closed. He is about to move on when Sharon's father bursts from the house, his face purpling with rage. "Pervert, slime ball," he screams. "Quit gawking at my daughter."*

*Jackson looks around for the object of the man's anger, but he's alone in the alley.*

*Sharon sits up and with the cruel bluntness of one accustomed to adulation, says peevishly, "Oh Daddy, don't be silly. It's only Jackson." And then she laughs, as though Jackson's humiliation is too funny for words. Her laughter is ten times worse than her father's blind cruelty. Clamping his lips together, Jackson stumbled away.*

Silence brought him back to the present. Anna Moffo no longer sang. Heaving himself from his chair, Jackson headed to his bedroom. Another long night lay ahead.

# 41

"Carol, I've decided to go to Portland Friday," Will said Tuesday afternoon.

"You haven't heard anything from the sheriff's office, I take it?"

"Only that the local police checked her usual hangouts with no result. Frankly, I believe a lot of Luce's friends would play dumb at sight of the uniform. That's why I think I should go."

After he left, Carol busied herself in the kitchen slicing vegetables for dinner. The phone rang as she was washing the chopping block. She set it on the counter, checked caller ID, and grabbed the receiver.

"Yes?"

"Carol? Dave here."

Her grip on the phone tightened. "Hi Dave, what's up?"

"Tom Malone made bail this morning. He pled not guilty at his initial hearing and waived his right to a jury trial. He's going to let the judge decide his case."

"Bail?" Carol looked out the window, feeling all at once exposed. "He's been free since this morning?" Dave had warned this might happen, but said she'd be notified at once. Right away, he'd said, not hours after the fact.

"Yes. I only found out myself. Seems the clerk got busy and dropped the ball. Malone's staying at a local motel with the young woman who paid his bail, the same young woman whose car he borrowed to come after you. The guy must have quite a line for her to stay with him after that." He cleared his throat. "Carol, I doubt Malone's stupid enough to put in an appearance at your place, but I want you to exercise caution."

She ran her tongue over suddenly dry lips before she spoke. "Thanks, Dave, I will." Hanging up, she found herself wondering if Tom was that stupid, if he could have gotten to Winter and into the house. Was he in the back bedroom, or upstairs in her room, waiting to surprise her? Stupid, letting her imagination run wild like this. Her gaze went to the carving knives in their wooden block. She pulled the biggest one out. Holding it tight, she reached for the phone.

# 42

Cora Newsome reminded Ben of a bird of prey. Hunched at the window, her oily black eyes followed Jackson Henry as he shepherded his little flock past the store.

"I can't stand that man," she said, moving back to the counter where Ben was ringing up two gallons of milk for Connor Murphy.

"Swear to god," Connor said, "my family goes through milk like most people breathe air. I brought two gallons home a couple of days ago, and here I am, buying two more."

Ignoring Connor, Cora went on talking. "He sneaks around and comes on folks without any warning. There's something not right about a man that size moving so silent."

She didn't see Connor's lips twitch, or the quick wink he threw Ben.

Ben, on the other hand, worked to keep his expression pleasant. Why couldn't Cora say something nice about someone for a change? He felt a certain amount of compassion for her, old and alone, but twenty years seemed too damn long to carry a grudge. He knew she'd start badmouthing Connor, too, the minute he left the store, using the same, worn out clichés: "He should be ashamed, keeping that wife of his pregnant all the time. They're like rabbits, and everyone knows they don't have a pot to pee in."

Ben threw in some licorice whips with the milk. "Tell those scallywags hello from Uncle Ben." He snapped his fingers. "Darn, I almost forgot. Hold on a sec, got a little something else for you."

Ignoring Cora's disgruntled "harrumph," Ben hurried down the hall, returning seconds later. He held out his hand, palm up. "Here, for your fly-tying."

Connor's eyes grew bright. "Son of a gun, Ben. Bronze herl. I was getting ready to order more."

"Made this myself," Ben said. "Read a tip on the Internet and decided to give it a try. Glad I did. Came out nicely, don't you think?"

Connor held the peacock quills up to the light. "Beautiful. How'd you get this color?"

Ben snorted. "So damn simple I don't know why I didn't think of it myself. Directions said to clip the quills to a line where they'd get good sun and turn 'em every day until the color was right. These took about three weeks."

Cora expelled a long-suffering sigh. "If you two are about done admiring those dirty feathers I'd like to pay for my bread and get home before sundown."

"Sorry, Cora," Ben said, and turned back to Connor. "I'd like to see how you use it."

"Thanks, Ben. You've inspired me. I may have to tie tonight. See you later." Connor tucked the quills into his shirt pocket, grabbed his purchases, and nodded at Cora. He left the store whistling.

Ignoring Cora's pursed lips and pissed-off glare, Ben ripped the paper receipt from the register and placed it with her bread.

He smiled. "Bye, Cora. Take care."

"Those feathers are unclean, Ben," she said. "And no doubt covered with lice. You shouldn't have them anywhere near food. Besides, they smell."

"That's not all that smells, Cora, dear," he muttered after the door closed behind her.

# 43

Calmer now, Carol waited outside for Will. She knew it unlikely Malone would come here after making bail. All the same, she didn't want to go through the house by herself.

While she waited, she wondered what Malone had in mind, waiving his right to a jury trial. Even if a judge dismissed his case, the college wouldn't take him back. Dave had called there and delivered the details of Malone's arrest and past history to no less than the President. Unlikely he'd find another position. If he traveled with his passport she supposed he could be on his way to Mexico by now. She doubted the county prosecutor would pursue the assault charges with more pressing concerns existing close to home.

Where did that leave her? If she'd learned anything, it was that Tom Malone did not give up. No matter how long it took, he'd find a way to finish what he started. She didn't want to spend her life looking over her shoulder but she had no intention of letting fear rule her life.

Right, Carol. That's why you're standing outside with a knife in your hand.

She breathed a sigh of relief when Will and Lady arrived.

Lady beat Will to her side. She licked Carol's hand before settling on her haunches.

"You okay?" Will said, taking her by the shoulders.

"I am now. In fact, I feel silly. This is probably the last place he'd come."

"Why don't you hand me that knife, then we'll make sure."

They started on the ground floor, checking James' bedroom, bathroom and utility room before taking the stairs to the loft. When they reached the landing, Will entered her bedroom before her. They checked the closet, the bathroom. Will took her arm. "Clear. Now let's take a look at the woodshed."

The woodshed also proved empty. They walked back to the house. Will took a seat on the deck. Lady sprawled at his feet. Carol went inside, poured two iced teas and took them back out.

After Will drained half his glass he set it down and leaned toward her. "I think you should stay with Rick and Lorrie while Malone's free."

Carol lifted her chin. "I won't let him chase me from my home."

"I figured you'd say that. So here's the alternate plan. Keep Lady here. You were going to keep her for me anyway when I went to Portland."

He reached down and patted Lady's head. "Lady will be fine. We have two more days of work when she'll ride with us. I'll check in with you over the weekend, too. She'll see me plenty."

Carol swallowed past the lump forming in her throat. "I don't know how to thank you, Will, for all you've done."

He grinned. "Thank me by promising you'll keep Lady at your side at all times, no matter what."

"Promise."

"One more thing. I asked Dave to post Malone's mug shot at the store. If the guy does decide to pay Winter a visit, he'll find a welcoming committee waiting." He stood up. "Now, finish your tea. We need to drive up to my place and get Lady's bed. I can't have my best girl sleeping on a hard floor."

*\*\**

The next morning Carol woke to find Lady's cold muzzle inches from her face.

"Morning, girl. I bet you're ready for a trip outside."

Lady's bark signaled agreement.

Keeping her promise to Will in mind, Carol waited on the porch until Lady came back inside. When she went to shower, Lady followed her up the stairs, toenails clicking on every step.

Carol emerged from the shower and nearly tripped over the dog, stretched across the doorway. "You're following orders, too, aren't you, sweetheart?"

Lady's stubby tail thumped against the tile.

\*\*\*

Two days flew by. Though she worked with Sarah, Lady never strayed. Whatever Carol did, weeding or watering or pushing an electric mower, Lady stayed beside her. She greeted Will joyfully in the morning and afternoon, but made no attempt to leave with him when he dropped Carol off or brought her home.

Friday morning, Carol dressed in denim shorts and a red sleeveless blouse tied at the waist, filled Lady's bowls, measured coffee grounds and put a bowl of oats in the microwave to cook.

While she ate, she thought about James' fly rod, waiting in the closet. She planned to spend part of her day practicing dry casting in the yard. She hadn't picked up a pole in two decades. Time she learned if she'd inherited any of her uncle's talent.

\*\*\*

Carol's first two tries ended in the lilac bushes. She was beginning to appreciate the amount of skill casting took. She reread the directions in her "How To" book. Tried a third cast, and decided she wasn't cut out for this. All this work to hook and play a fish until it was too exhausted to struggle. Her uncle had been big on catch and release, but she doubted the fish considered it sport.

A shadow fell over the page. Puzzled, Carol looked up, surprised to see a dark cloud spreading like a bruise over the blue sky. A puff of wind came off the hill and riffled the pages of her book. Lady raised her muzzle and sniffed.

The sudden absence of sound should have warned her. Not an insect buzzed, clicked, or hummed. Not a bird sang or swooped or dived. On the hill, the still pines appeared carved from stone. Another, stronger gust of wind came, bringing a powerful tang of ozone. The crowns on the locust trees swelled to twice their size. Lady whined and pushed against Carol's knees. When the fine hairs on her arms stirred, Carol grabbed book and fishing rod and ran for the house. She and Lady reached the porch an instant before a blinding flash turned the landscape to neon. A simultaneous clap of thunder rocked the ground and the floorboards beneath her feet. Lady barked, and when Carol opened the door, the dog refused to move until Carol stepped inside.

From the window, Carol watched lightning bolt from clouds that boiled and bubbled like a witch's cauldron. With each crack of thunder the house shuddered. Day became night. Wind moaned through the trees like a woman bereaved. Peering through the gloom, Carol saw several pines snap in half, the severed trunks falling end over end to the ground. The smoke detector gave a high bleep, and the power went out. A large branch blew out of the darkness and slammed against the window. Carol ducked, expecting glass to shatter. It didn't, but after that, she took refuge under the staircase, sitting on the floor with her knees drawn up and her arm around Lady's neck.

Fifteen minutes later, the sky cleared. The wind died. Sunlight kindled the pines with gold fire. Her yard lay buried under a foot of leaves. She counted at least six broken pines on the hill, and wondered if any had fallen across her road. Then she thought of Rick and Lorrie. They lived further up the canyon and their yard was filled with tall, old trees. Had they weathered the storm? She picked up the phone. No dial tone. The lines were down.

# 44

For the first time, Will wished cell phones worked in the canyon. With the phones out he couldn't call Carol to see how she weathered the storm. There was no question she'd be safe inside the house. James had been smart, planting trees around his place but never close enough to pose any danger from wind or fire.

Will surveyed the mess in his yard and called himself lucky. Had the wind come from a different direction, the uprooted cottonwood now covering his front yard might have fallen on, or through, his roof. A few hours with his chainsaw seemed a small price to pay for that luck. Too bad though. He'd miss its shade, and Cora would miss sitting beneath its branches when she visited. Her attachment to the spot had struck him as odd until he noticed the initials carved in the trunk and realized the tree reminded her of happier times. The day that happiness ended remained engraved on his mind.

From the age of fourteen to sixteen, he mowed the Newsome's lawn, thanks to Roger Newsome who knew how much

Will needed the work. Cora hadn't been too happy about the arrangement, and once he heard her arguing with Roger about letting 'Zabransky trash" near their home. "How do you know he won't steal from us," she'd challenged. Will, working around the corner of the house, had flushed with shame and anger. He wasn't a Zabransky and he wasn't trash. He'd been tempted then to quit, but he needed the money, and Mr. Newsome had hired him, not Cora. After that day, he made sure to stay out of her way, though he knew her eyes followed him from the time he came to the moment he left. That day, a Thursday, he changed clothes as soon as he got home from school and headed to their house. He arrived to find Cora sitting on the porch, her face and blouse spattered with what at first he thought must be spaghetti sauce but soon recognized was blood.

He remembered standing mute while Cora stared at him, or past him or through him. Will couldn't tell for sure because her eyes were unfocused and not tracking well. In shock, he realized later.

"Mrs. Newsome, are you hurt? Should I call Mr. Newsome?"

"He's gone, Will. He isn't coming back," she said.

Even though he didn't like her, he couldn't help feeling sorry for her. What hurt most, though, was that Roger Newsome, whom he respected and admired, had beaten his wife. He was no different than his stepfather, Ray.

"I'm sorry, Mrs. Newsome," he said.

"So am I," she said. "So am I," she said again, her voice growing hard.

Will mowed the grass. He didn't know what else to do. When Cora came to pay him, her face was clean. She'd changed into a fresh housedress that clung to a figure still trim in middle age. Will noticed that she'd buttoned it all the way to her neck.

Like his mother, Cora wanted her bruises kept hidden.

"Thank you, Will,' she said, placing a ten in his hand. "I won't need you after this. I hope you understand."

Will did. Cora had her pride. He'd seen her at her weakest, and she couldn't tolerate that. Besides, with Roger gone, she no longer had to tolerate 'Zabransky trash.'

The screech of a hawk ended Will's reverie. He blew out a sigh, shook off the past, and went to the tool shed for his chainsaw.

Three hours later, he cut the last branch from the massive trunk. He turned off the saw, used his forearm to wipe sweat from his face, and peered into the gaping hole where the tree once stood. He'd plant another, maybe a dogwood, or a redbud, one that blossomed in the spring.

A scrap of paper or maybe a bit of cloth caught in the churned earth caught his eye. Curious, he bent down and reached for it.

"What in hell?" Will brought the thing in his hands closer to his face and the bottom dropped out of his stomach.

# 45

Ben reached into the freezer. "Good thing I purchased that generator when I did," he said over his shoulder. "Just hope I have enough ice to go around."

"I imagine the power will come back on before nightfall," Cora said. "The ice will keep things in my little freezer frozen until then."

Ben straightened – a bag in each hand – and turned as Connor Murphy burst through the door and set the bell jangling.

"There's trouble at Will's. Police cars, an ambulance –"

"Whoa, Connor," Ben ordered. "Stop. Take a breath. What's this about Will?"

Connor pulled off his cap and slapped it against his leg. "I was coming from the Wright's – I helped Joe and Lureen clean up after the storm – and I saw an ambulance turn into Will's. I followed it, in case, in case –"

"Connor," Ben warned. "Get to the point, man."

"I saw Dave. I didn't see Will. I asked Dave what was going on. He told me to leave."

Ben dropped the ice to the floor. "Will's hurt?"

"Maybe the ambulance came for that woman," Cora said. "Luce. I bet she came crawling back to Will ten times the worse for wear."

Connor ignored her. "That big old cottonwood came down in the storm. It darn near covers Will's yard." He studied his hat as though he'd never seen it before. "You don't suppose Will got caught underneath?"

Cora's gasp came loud in the stricken silence that followed. The blood drained from her face. Even her lips turned white.

"Connor!" Ben started around the counter. "Quick, give me a hand."

"Cora," Ben said when they reached her. "Let us help you into a chair."

"I'm sorry, Mrs. Newsome," Connor said. "I didn't mean to upset −"

Cora cut him off. "I'm fine. Don't bother yourselves." She shrugged their hands away.

She wasn't fine, Ben knew. Her arm, under his hand, felt cold as the ice in his freezer.

"Let Connor drive you home, Cora. I'll drive to Will's and find out what's going on."

"I don't need Connor to drive me across the road, thank you." She smiled at Ben. "Will used to mow our lawn. Did you know that?"

"No. No, I didn't." Her smile made him uneasy. He saw no pleasure in it.

"I didn't want him around, I called him trash. I was wrong. He wasn't a bad boy. He worked hard."

Ben never considered Cora frail, but now she appeared so fragile, so brittle, he thought she might shatter. He reached again for her arm, but the moment he touched her, the old Cora resurfaced. Her eyes flashed a warning. "I said I'm fine, Ben."

The moment the door closed behind her, Ben turned to Connor. "Make sure she gets home. I'm going to Will's."

\*\*\*

Ben passed the ambulance on its way to Pendleton, siren off, and traveling within the speed limit. That meant one of three things he decided: no occupant or, occupant with minor injuries or – and dread nearly choked him – the occupant inside was beyond help.

"Not Will," he muttered under his breath. "Hasn't he had enough grief?" Ben wasn't thinking only of the young wife Will lost, but the stories he'd heard from Rick about Will's stepfather, the beatings, neglect, and daily humiliations. What manner of God allowed children to suffer so? A God he had no use for – that was for sure.

He met Dave coming from Will's drive. They braked at the same time.

Ben looked at the deputy, afraid to ask.

Dave understood. "Will's fine," he said. "He can tell you about it. I have to be somewhere."

Ben whistled when he saw the huge stack of branches in Will's yard. He found his friend sitting on the stairs of his deck, twisting a twig in his hands, his face unreadable.

"Connor stopped at the store," Ben said, by way of greeting. He clapped Will on the back. "God, Will, when I passed that ambulance...." He drew a shaky breath. "I'm glad you're okay."

"I'm pretty sure Roger Newsome is in that ambulance," Will said, "or what's left of him."

"Roger? Cora's Roger? What the hell?"

"I found him." Will jerked his chin toward the edge of the yard. "Buried near the tree."

Shock drove the air from Ben's lungs. He struggled to suck it back in. "Jesus, Will. Cora was in the store when Connor burst in and told us the ambulance was here. He mentioned the tree, thought you might have been underneath when the wind took it down."

Will methodically stripped bark from the twig. "Dave's headed to Cora's now." He threw the twig away. "My God, Ben, she carried that secret all these years. When I think of her coming here, sitting under that tree..." Will shuddered. "I felt sorry for her. She was always a hard woman to like but I've tried because I remember how much she loved Roger and what losing him did to her. How could she live with that secret all these years?"

Ben shook his head. "I don't know, Will. I don't know."

# 46

D ave stood in Cora's bedroom. The gun, free from her hand, lay on the pillow beside her. Blue flowers, hand-embroidered, edged the pillow case. Only a small trickle of blood spilled from her temple.

Dave studied the silver-framed photo of Cora and Roger that rested in the crook of her arm. The radiant girl in the picture bore no resemblance to the woman on the bed.

The scene reminded him of the Faulkner story he read in high school. At least Cora buried Roger, instead of sleeping next to him all those years.

He had found her confession under the salt shaker on her kitchen table. That damn silly salt shaker shaped like a mushroom in her spotless little kitchen with yellow and white checked curtains at the windows. Dave drew a shaky breath. God, he hated this. He took his eyes from Cora, let them travel around the pale pink walls of her room, the sheer white curtains gathered at the windows, and fought to make sense of it all. "Maybe I'm in the wrong line of work," he said into the silence. His eyes slid back to

Cora before he turned to go. He'd wait outside for the forensics team, outside in the fresh air.

\*\*\*

Cora and what remained of Roger Newsome, were buried in a cemetery behind a church almost as old as Winter. A black iron fence surrounded the plot and on either side of the gate a fountain of forsythia grew. Morning lent a soft glow to the oldest headstones, many dating back to the late 1800's. No grass grew here, but buttercups had sprung up everywhere, and the distant Blue Mountains stood sharp against a cornflower blue sky.

Ben, Rick, Jackson, and Will had dug the graves the previous day. Donations collected at Ben's store paid for simple pine coffins adorned by Lorrie and Lureen Wright with garden flowers and boughs of fresh pine.

Joe Wright, wearing a dark green corduroy jacket shiny with age, delivered their eulogy.

"I was Roger's best man at their wedding." He paused. A smile played on his mouth.

As he talked of growing up with Cora and Roger, Carol looked around the cemetery. Many of the graves had no headstones, only square markers held in the ground by metal stakes. On some, mementos left by visiting family and friends told their own story, like the one nearest her with its glass canning jar weighted with stones. Inside were sewing thimbles, a small pair of orange-handled scissors, and five spools of sun-faded thread. On the next grave over, plastic roses filled a pail, a miniature spade and trowel wired to the stems. Toy trucks on another revealed their own sad story.

Her attention came back to Joe, stepping forward to stand between the two coffins. He rested a hand on each.

"Cora. Roger. You're at peace now. Our thoughts go with you."

Only the high whine of a passing jet broke the silence that followed. Joe stepped back and nodded to the pallbearers.

The coffins were lowered into the earth. Joe took a handful of dirt and cast it upon them, after which he held a shovel filled with dirt so others could do the same.

The men, working in twos, filled in the graves. Even the youngest boys took their turn with the shovels.

Carol, standing with Sarah and Lorrie, thought how different country burials were. Instead of backhoes wielded by strangers, friends dug the grave with shovels. Instead of waiting to bury the deceased until the mourners left, friends lowered the coffin, filled in the grave and smoothed the last bit of earth over the top. There was comfort to be taken in this, a sense of completeness and letting go.

\*\*\*

In the cemetery surrounded by gravestones, he can't help but think of Alec. He doesn't know where his brother is buried. He tried to find out after he was on his own, but fate wasn't through playing with him. The records he needed from Social Services had been destroyed by a flood. He checked with the Department of Vital Statistics in Salem for a death certificate and was told it had been misfiled. "We'll keep looking," the clerk said, but he could tell she didn't mean it.

Alec. No one spoke of him or of their mother after that terrible night, after he became a ward of the state.

Ron and Kayla Ross became his foster parents. Good people. They opened their arms to a scared, guilt-ridden child and loved him unconditionally. Within weeks, his stutter all but disappeared. He stopped crying himself to sleep every night.

Then Ron died in a freak accident at his construction site and Kayla, dazed by grief, became a walking zombie, unable to cope with her own two children, let alone him and their other foster child, Glenda.

He went to the Blewitts: George, a tall, beady-eyed and balding man with a heavy hand, Amelia, his short, fat, merry-eyed wife. Her eyes grew far merrier when George found it necessary to punish one of the children.

The man shudders, remembering their cat. They took better care of it than they did of their four foster children. The boy had been sick to his stomach after he bashed its head against the side of the house one night, but lighter, too, as though some of his rage and loneliness died with the small creature. The feeling didn't last.

Not when the Blewitts went after Billy.

Five years old, a little slow, Billy reminded him of Alec. He had the same trusting, puppy-dog look in his eyes, the same hopeful smile.

That look brought out the worst in the Blewitts.

His last day in their household began with a loud screech from Amelia. "Goddam little brat, you did it on purpose."

Billy, once again, wet his bed.

The kids were forced to watch Billy being dragged from the bedroom, naked and shivering.

George took his time loosening his belt. Amelia's eyes moistened in anticipation.

When the police arrived, summoned by a hysterical Amelia, George Blewitt stood bent over the kitchen sink, an icepack held to his broken nose. The bite mark on Amelia's cheek required a trip to the emergency room, several stitches, antibiotics and a tetanus shot.

The children, except for him, were transferred to other foster families. Even though his violence was considered justified, the Court ruled he needed a more disciplined setting.

He went to the Schofield Home for Boys.

Schofield had been a summer camp compared to the Blewitt's.

Pebbles mixed with dirt struck the coffins and rattled across the wood, forcing him back to the present. The man held back a sigh and stepped up for his turn with the shovel.

# 47

"Good grief," Carol said. "Who's going to eat all this?"

"Don't worry," Lorrie said, setting a sweet potato casserole on the oil-cloth covered table. "If I know Rick, he'll sample every dish and come back for seconds."

Carol hadn't thought she was hungry, but seeing so much food – macaroni and cheese, grilled salmon, fried chicken, and ham – made her mouth water Add potato salad, beans swimming in barbecue sauce, scalloped potatoes, homemade bread with pots of butter and finally, pies – huckleberry, apple, rhubarb – and it was all she could do not to reach for a plate and dig in. She did manage to wait until the line dwindled before she served herself. She carried her meal to a lawn chair at the edge of the yard and sat down. For a moment, she closed her eyes, savoring the warmth of the sun on her face, the faint scent of lilacs coming from bushes near the fence.

"Not being anti-social, are we?"

Carol opened her eyes as Lorrie took a seat across from her.

"No. Just enjoying the weather. I suppose I should feel bad about Cora, but I like to think she's at peace now, and Roger, too."

"Poor Roger." Lorrie said. A fleeting sadness crossed her face. "Mom used to say Cora loved him too hard. Suffocated him with love, was the way she put it. Maybe he'd had enough and tried to leave."

"We'll never know."

Lorrie nodded and began eating. "Damn," she said. "This potato salad is good, even if I did make it myself."

Carol laughed. "Good thing you have long arms, makes it easy to pat yourself on the back."

Ignoring the jibe, Lorrie moved on. "I just came from talking to Sarah. She's going to keep working for Will after her school term ends."

"Yes. Will mentioned she might. With all the other excitement, I forgot to tell you."

Lorrie's gaze slipped over Carol's shoulder. "Here comes Ben. Doesn't he look smashing in that shirt?"

Ben reached them before Carol could turn to look.

"How are my two favorite women?"

"Shame on you, Ben Wagner." Lorrie shook her fork at him. "I heard you say those exact words to at least three other women at the buffet table."

He grinned. "Caught. What can I say? You're all my favorites."

"In that case, you're forgiven. I saw you talking to my husband. What were you yakking about? Wait. Don't tell me. Trout or steelhead?"

Ben's eyes sparkled. "I asked Rick if he wanted to go fishing later this evening. He passed."

Lorrie was right, Carol thought. Ben did look handsome in that shirt, an almost cobalt blue that matched his eyes.

"Good thing," Lorrie said. "My plans for him tonight do not include fishing."

His eyebrows shot up. His eyes grew even brighter. "Intriguing remark. Care to elaborate?"

Lorrie winked at him and changed the subject. "So, what do you think of our Sarah staying on for the summer?"

"I didn't know she was," Ben said. "What, is she bringing Brandon here?"

"No. You know Grace has health problems and Sarah doesn't want to disrupt Brandon's routine. He's happy with his grandma and it's only for six more weeks."

"Too bad. I'd like to meet the little guy. I could take him fishing."

Rick, arriving with Will and Sarah, overheard. "What little guy?"

"Brandon." Ben pulled a lawn chair close and motioned Sarah into it. "Lorrie tells me you're extending your stay with us this year." He smiled down at her. "Working for Will must have its good points."

"It does," Sarah nodded. "The best one is money. Tuition goes up again this fall." She hesitated. "Actually, there's another reason I'm staying. Aunt Grace has several doctor visits coming up. I want to make sure she's okay before I take off."

"I bet Dave has nothing to do with this decision." A smile tugged the corners of Ben's mouth.

Sarah's copper skin turned rosy. A dimple in her left cheek deepened.

"Jackson isn't here," Ben said, casting a look around. "Isn't he coming?"

"No." Lorrie said. "He told me he had to get home and finish an order. He did his bit helping with the burial."

"I always wondered why Cora was so rude to such a nice guy."

"I don't think Cora needed a reason," Rick answered.

"You're right, Honey." Lorrie glanced at Rick. "Remember when we were kids? Roger always had time for us. He'd ask how we were doing in school, or if we'd been fishing and how many we caught. She'd be hanging on his arm like she thought we were trying to steal him away."

"I think I saw her right after she shot him." Will's announcement, spoken with complete calm, took a moment to sink in.

Lorrie's fork clattered to her plate. "Say again?"

"You remember, I mowed their yard when I was a kid." His hands went to the back of Carol's chair. "The last day I worked, Cora was on the porch. She had had blood on her face and blouse."

One of his hands found Carol's shoulder, gave it a small squeeze. "I thought Roger had hit her. I can't tell you how awful I felt, or how betrayed. I really liked him." He shook his head. "It never occurred to me the blood was his, or that his body was probably inside the house."

"Jesus, Will," Ben breathed. "And I thought I'd heard everything."

"Does Dave know?" Lorrie asked. "That you were there?"

"Sure. I had no reason to keep it from him."

"This has all the earmarks of a bad TV movie," Ben said, attempting to lighten their mood. "You know a," he made air quotes with his fingers, "'docudrama,' based on real events. Did this beautiful woman kill her husband, or did she convince the handsome yard boy to do it for her?"

"Not funny, Ben." Rick's voice carried an edge.

Ben heard it. "Hey, I'm sorry, but it did happen a long time ago. I apologize, Will. It was tactless of me."

Dave's arrival eased the awkward moment. The talk switched to the storm and the damage it caused.

When that topic exhausted itself, Rick turned to Ben. "I hear Joe took a fourteen-inch rainbow from that hole below his place the other day."

Ben appeared relieved that Rick was no longer upset with him. "I was thinking some place closer to home this evening."

"Wish I could go," Dave said, "but we're a man short tonight so I'm pulling a second shift." He reached for Sarah's hand. "How about meeting me around nine for my dinner break?"

Seeing the shine in Sarah's eyes, Carol thought her friend might as well hang a sign around her neck – I love Dave.

"Sure," Sarah said, "that leaves me plenty of time to make dinner for uncle and auntie and clean up afterward." She turned to Lorrie. "Is it okay if I take a piece of that berry pie home? The pie is for Uncle Louie," she hastened to add.

Lorrie snorted. "Take a whole pie. Take two or three. Save Rick from himself."

"What?"

Lorrie ignored him. "Take some chicken, too, and there are salads no one's even sampled yet. You and Grace won't have to cook for days."

Dave leaned down, kissed Sarah's cheek and shook hands with everyone. "I've got to get a move on." He looked at Will. "A minute?"

"Sure."

They watched the two men walk to Dave's car and begin talking. Will at one point folded his arms over his chest and nodded. Dave clapped him on the shoulder and got into his cruiser.

Ben turned to Sarah with a smile. "Don't be sad, little one. You'll see him again this evening."

Everyone laughed. Sarah blushed again.

# 48

After the funeral luncheon, Ben returned home but left the *Closed* sign in the store window. He made a quick inventory of his stock, set the backyard sprinkler on a timer, and made a mental note to prune one of the trees before it got completely out of control. Then he got ready to hit the river. Maybe later he'd go into town for a meal; a movie too, if there was anything worth seeing.

He'd laid his gear on the bed: vest, hat, bamboo rod, the small metal case containing his favorite flies. His waders sat on the floor.

He was glad now that he was going solo. After his stupid gaffe at the luncheon, he craved quiet. What in hell had he been thinking, making that crack about Will and Cora? Rick might have been the one to shut him up, but it was the hurt in Will's eyes that had really silenced him.

Ben slipped on a tan chamois shirt and sat down to don waterproof socks. He laced up his sneakers, stood, and slipped into his vest, grabbed hat, fishing rod and waders and headed for the stairs. He'd take his car instead of the pickup, since he could park on the side of the road and walk to his spot.

\*\*\*

Dave sat behind his desk, his impatience growing. He glanced at his watch again. Sarah promised to call when she reached home. Shouldn't take her more than twenty minutes, but thirty-five had passed and still no call. She'd left a few minutes past ten, after they shared his dinner break in her pickup. Not that he worried about her getting home safely, he just wanted to hear her voice again.

Okay, he decided, reaching for the phone. He'd call her; maybe lecture her a little about keeping her word.

Sarah's Aunt Grace answered.

"No, Sarah isn't home yet, Dave."

Did he detect amusement in her voice?

"Most likely she's driving slower than usual," Grace said. You know how thick the deer are this time of night. When did she leave you?"

Dave told her, and her soft laughter, so like Sarah's, came down the line.

"It's barely been twenty minutes, Dave. I'm sure she'll arrive any minute now."

"You're probably right," Dave said, hoping Grace didn't think him as foolish as he felt. "Would you ask her to call when she gets in? I'd like to say good night."

"I'll do that, Dave, I'll have her call. You take care now."

Ten minutes later the phone shrilled again. Grace put her beadwork aside and smiled at Louis. "My goodness, Dave's as bad as you used to be."

Louis, half asleep with an open book in his lap, grunted.

"Hello again, Dave. Oh, Ben. I'm sorry, I expected someone else."

Louis, suddenly alert, set his book aside and joined her at the phone.

"No, Sarah's not here. Where? A flat tire? Hold on, Ben, I'll let you talk to Louis."

Wordlessly, she handed her husband the phone and pressed against him, listening as best she could to the one-sided conversation.

"No, she isn't home yet," Louis said. "Perhaps someone offered to drive her back to Dave. Thanks for calling, Ben. I'm going to give Dave a call. I'm sure Sarah's okay."

Grace gripped his arm. Louis held up his hand, the phone still pressed to his ear.

"No, Ben," he said, "that won't be necessary. You stay put. I'll call you after I talk to Dave."

Louis hung up and turned to Grace. "Ben found Sarah's pickup with a flat parked near the railroad crossing. I'm sure she got a lift with someone, she could be back with Dave by now." Louis appeared only a little concerned when he picked up the phone again and punched in Dave's number.

But Grace Blue Hawk experienced a sudden, overwhelming dread.

# 49

The phone wakened Carol from sleep. Midnight, read the bedside clock. She fumbled for the receiver when she saw Will's name on the ID

"What is it? Have you heard from Luce?"

"Sarah's missing."

Carol fought to shake the cobwebs from her brain. "What?"

"Dave just called. She left him more than two hours ago, after they spent his dinner hour together. Her pickup was found, but no sign of her. I'm getting ready to meet Dave. I can stop for you on the way – that is, if you want to come."

"Absolutely. I'll be ready."

Lady whined and pushed her cold nose into Carol's hand. "Yes, girl, you're coming, too."

Carol crawled out of bed and slipped into jeans and a cotton sweater. She looked out the window. A clear night, with a wisp of cloud veiling the moon.

She padded into the bathroom and splashed cold water on her face, feeling rough ridges of scar tissue beneath her hand.

Had Sarah left her pickup to walk home in the dark? She was so small, so light. A car veering toward the shoulder could ... a driver might not even realize.... Carol forced the image away and bent to tie her sneakers.

\*\*\*

Blue and white flashers on official vehicles threw the landscape into stuttering patterns of light and dark. Will parked well back from all the activity, grabbed his flashlight from under the seat, and walked with Carol to find Dave, Lady padding silently with them. They found him talking with Grace and Louis. Carol thought Dave looked like a man sucker-punched and kicked hard on his way down. Anguish swam in Grace's dark eyes. Louis' face revealed nothing, but his hands, clenched at his sides, betrayed his distress. Wordlessly, Carol hugged Grace, felt the slight woman's arms tighten around her. Louis nodded, unclenching one hand to take Will's. Carol turned to Dave, but the desolation in his eyes was so great it rendered her mute. Another deputy approached, pulled him aside, and said a few words too low to hear. Dave nodded, then turned back to Louis and Grace. He reached for Grace's hand, but directed his words to both. "You need to go home now. You need to be there in case Sarah calls. I promise to let you know the minute we learn anything."

Carol saw the war going on behind their eyes. They wanted to stay. Grace, face lined with fatigue, stood tall at her husband's side. Louis, his face set in stern lines, finally nodded. With Dave accompanying them, they walked back to their car.

The crackle of radios disturbed the night's stillness. A low hum of voices came from the tree-dotted field where flashlight beams pierced the deep shadows of the tree-dotted field that lay beyond the road. Hearing a familiar voice, Carol turned and saw Rick talking with Sheriff McReady and two officers in tribal police uniforms, a man and a woman.

Carol realized Sarah had gone missing on Reservation land. That meant FBI involvement too, if she didn't turn up soon.

She watched McReady speak to the male officer, who nodded, walked to his patrol car, and drove off, headed upriver.

Rick explained when he joined them a moment later.

"I told the sheriff about Luce's experience with that guy from the camp, the one who picked her up then didn't want to let her go. He's sending a man up to the camp to ask a few questions." Rick glanced at Dave, at the Blue Hawk's car, and lowered his voice, though Dave remained well out of hearing. "What if a carload of those guys came upon Sarah walking alone?"

Nausea surged in Carol's throat. She swallowed it back. "Oh, God, Rick, you don't think....?"

Rick shrugged. "Better to check it out now rather than later."

Spotlights shone on Sarah's little red pickup, now cordoned off with yellow tape. Jackson and Ben stood outside the tape, Jackson with his hands balled into his pockets, rocked on his feet. Ben, still as stone, watched a man and woman go over the interior with flashlights.

After Louis and Grace departed, Dave gathered everyone together. Volunteers were separated into two groups, each accompanied by a deputy or tribal policeman. They would take opposite sides of the road, searching for any sign, paying particular attention to the ditches.

Two hours passed before Dave called everyone back in. "There's nothing more we can do tonight. We'll start again at first light."

Rick stepped forward and addressed Dave. "We'll be here. Try to get some rest yourself. You won't be any good to Sarah if you're too strung out to think straight."

Fear had sucked the lifeblood from Dave, leaving a hollow-eyed stranger in his place. "Christ." His voice shook. "This is a fucking nightmare; it doesn't make any sense."

"I know Dave, he won't leave," Will said on their way back to the pickup. "He sure as hell won't get any rest."

"Can't the sheriff force him to leave?" Carol said.

Will drove slowly, alert for deer and nocturnal creatures. "McReady's a good guy. He knows Dave can't stop looking any more than he can. He's letting Dave run the show while he stays in the background, but he's got Dave's back all the way." His headlights picked out a possum inching across the pavement. He guided the truck around it. "Sarah wouldn't get into a car with a stranger, no matter how far she had to walk," he said. "Not unless she was forced."

He drove in silence after that, until they crossed the bridge and came to her house turnoff. "That talk I had with Dave earlier today?"

Carol had wondered. "What about it?"

"He wanted to let me know the Portland police got a call from one of Luce's friends. Guy said he thinks he saw her a couple of days ago."

"But that's good news, Will. Why didn't you tell me?"

"Because Dave said not to put much faith in it. When the guy found out there was no reward, he hung up."

"I'm sorry." Carol couldn't bring herself to ask the question that preyed on her mind, now that Sarah was missing. She had a hunch the same question preyed on Will's.

Had Luce left Winter on her own, or had she been taken?

# 50

Elation threatens to send him off the road. He'd wanted to yell, "I have her," and let the echo bounce through the canyon. Talk about serendipity.

He had driven over the railroad tracks and his headlight spotted her pickup. As soon as she recognized him she got out, holding her useless cell phone in the air, a rueful grin on her full lips, those perfect white teeth gleaming in the starlit dark.

"Darn thing." She shook the phone. "Doesn't work here."

He swore he'd never hunt on home ground; a rule he'd strictly enforced until recently. Hell, this wasn't hunting. This was fate delivering the deserving into his hands.

"I promised to call Dave when I got home."

That delightful, throaty little voice of hers. God, he'd wanted to take her right there! Of course, if anyone had happened along as he helped her into his car, she'd be safe now. But no one happened along. She asked to use his phone when they got inside his home. He waited until she began to dial, and grabbed her from behind. She never had a chance. The look in her eyes when he had her bound and gagged. Christ! It had taken all his self-control to keep his hands off her. Dangerous? Yes. But God, this feeling! Like champagne bubbling in his veins. No. Champagne is cold. This feels like liquid heat, molten lead, a strange, exquisite alchemy taking place as it burns a fiery path through his body. Sarah is no different from the others.

# 51

Will walked Carol to the door and saw her inside.

Lady turned a couple of circles on the rug and settled down, her eyes steady on both of them.

"You won't get much sleep." Will's earlier taut mask had been replaced by dark circles under his eyes. "Daylight's only a few hours away. I'll come back for you in the morning."

Carol knew she might come to regret what she was about to do, but tonight was a grim reminder of how chance snatched happiness away without conscience or consideration. She didn't want to be alone. She didn't want to be without Will.

"Stay. There's no sense in your driving home. You'll get a few extra minutes of sleep, at least." Looking into his dark eyes was like falling into a well with no bottom in sight.

"If I stay I don't think I'll be thinking of sleep."

"Me neither." Did she say the words, or only think them? Carol reached for his hand and drew him inside.

He kissed her forehead, her cheeks, and the corners of her mouth. He undressed her with such tenderness her eyes pricked with tears. His fingers counted each rib, each knob in her spine, before tracing the line of her neck, the length of her thigh. His touch made her new. She became light as air, soft as sunlight, reborn in a dizzying world they created together.

Even in sleep, Will held her close. Carol wanted to hold on to these moments as long as possible. She shifted her head and he stirred, mumbled something unintelligible, and tightened his hold. Beneath her cheek, his heart beat strong and steady.

She should tell him. Her cowardly self insisted nothing could be served by revealing the truth, not after all this time. Don't risk it, that same self said. She feared his disappointment more than she feared Tom Malone.

She wished dawn were light years away.

***

"It's time." Will's breath tickling her ear; his warm hand stroking her back.

Carol forced her eyes open; unable to believe she had slept after all.

"I need to run home and change." He kissed her shoulder. "I'll be back soon."

She sat up, pulling the sheet around her, suddenly awkward.

He pulled her back down on the bed, wrapping his arms around her. "No regrets, I hope."

She whispered the lie into his shoulder. "None."

She and Lady followed him downstairs. Lady went outside with him, but at his command, returned to the house. Carol started coffee and went upstairs to shower and dress. Standing beneath the shower, Will's, 'no regrets, I hope,' came back to her. Not since they met had they spoken of the day at the creek with his stepfather. She had lied to him then, gone on living the lie until she believed the truth no longer mattered. She'd never expected to see Will again. She bowed her head beneath the cascade of hot water and let the memory find her, a memory that refused to die in spite of time and how hard she fought to erase it.

*They planned to meet at the creek but the morning was almost gone and Will still hadn't called. Finally, a little after eleven, she heard from him.*

*"Ray's been drinking and I didn't want to leave Mom, but he's gone now, took off for town with two other buddies. He won't come back until it's time to sober up for his next shift."*

*"So you can get away?"*

*"Yes, I'll meet you at the swimming hole."*

*They swam where a small waterfall emptied into a deep pool, treading water while it washed over their heads and shoulders. They floated on their backs holding hands. They didn't talk, shy and awkward with this new feeling that had grown between them. Afterwards they climbed to a grassy rise above the creek. Will spread their towels and stretched out beside her, his elbow planted on the ground, his head balanced on his hand so he could look down at her. They did that a lot, this staring.*

When Will leaned down to kiss her, Carol knew she would remember the sweetness of the moment for the rest of her life.

Then Ray stumbled out of the trees clutching a half-empty bottle of whiskey. He saw them and halted, stupefied. "Well, I'll be fucked. Didn't know you had it in you, boy."

Will rose, pulling her up with him. "Go home, Carol. Now."

"No, Carol," Ray said. "Don't go. The party's just getting started. Crummy friends dumped me when they found out I was broke, but this is better than any trip to town."

He lurched toward them. Carol's feet refused to move. She couldn't leave Will alone with this...this...drooling monstrosity.

Ray tried shoving Will aside.

"Stay away from her," Will said.

Ray laughed.

Will threw a punch, but Ray, no stranger to barroom brawls, ducked, dropped his bottle to the grass, and shot his fist out, connecting with Will's face. Will went down, blood streaming from his mouth and nose.

Carol screamed when Ray's steel-toed work boot connected with the side of Will's head. She saw his eyes roll up before he went limp.

She tried to reach him, but Ray grabbed her. One grimy hand clamped over her mouth, the other tore at her bathing suit.

He pushed her down, forced his knee between her legs. His face loomed above her, slick with sweat, his eyes red-rimmed, the *whites shot with broken blood vessels. Carol felt a tearing pain and screamed against his hand.*

*An eternity passed before Ray's weight left her. "Tell anyone about this and I'll kill that little bastard," he said, zipping his fly. His eyes flicked to Will. He wiped his mouth with the back of his hand, grinned, and nudged Will with the toe of his boot. "I mean it."*

*After he left, Carol crawled to the creek and submerged herself, desperate to wash away the pain and filth and shame.*

*She got back to Will as he was coming around.*

*"Did he hurt you?" Will's first thought, his first words*

*"No, he got scared when you passed out. He ran off." She used her towel to wipe the blood from his face. "You need a doctor, Will. Your nose looks broken and you were unconscious, you need to get your head checked."*

*"I need to get you home and check on Mom. There's no telling what Ray might do to her when he's like this."*

Carol forced the memory away. Will would be here soon. There was no time to agonize over the past. She had believed Ray. She had kept the secret. She turned off the water and reached for a towel. Finding Sarah was all that mattered.

A spasm of guilt seized her. When she lay in Will's arms, she hadn't thought of Sarah at all.

# 52

The man studies Sarah by lamp glow. Her small, perfect body, the spill of hair that appears almost blue with reflected light. Soon he must rejoin the others in a search he alone knows is futile.

God, she's beautiful! She tastes beautiful, too, like sun-ripened blackberries picked from the vine. And she's a fighter. He expected a fight from the other one, had been disappointed by how quickly she surrendered. But Sarah! Her flat gaze gives no quarter. She can't hold back the cries of pain, but her eyes hold only contempt. Unsettling. He wonders if the control he so prides himself on has begun to slip, if he's heading toward his own destruction. No. He can't allow himself to think that way. He's tired, that's all. He's had very little sleep since she fell into his arms.

One more day. He feels sure he can safely keep her at least that long. He is by no means finished here. Besides, he can't dispose of her until the search ends.

He fingers the teeth marks on her belly. Leaning down, he plants soft kisses on them.

"You should see Dave's face, Sarah."

She stares at the ceiling, revealing nothing.

He doesn't care for insolence though, and leaves her with a parting gift; a little something to remember until his return.

She shows her appreciation with a choked scream.

He sings a few bars of "Celeste Aida" in the shower as he soaps her scent from his body. Walled in by water, he thinks his voice sounds very much like the late, great, Mario Lanza.

Now there was a man beset by demons.

# 53

Dave's uniform was a roadmap of wrinkles. Red threaded the whites of his eyes and darkness bruised the skin beneath them. The carefree young man Carol met at Will's barbecue no longer existed. Only finding Sarah, alive and well, could bring him back.

Baldwin confirmed what Will predicted hours before. Dave had not left the scene, nor had he slept.

Louis had returned alone and sat in his car, head back, eyes closed.

Ben and Jackson were also back, waiting where they both stood before, outside the yellow tape around Sarah's pickup.

A lanky, saturnine-faced man in a grey suit leaned against a dark blue sedan, talking to a tribal policeman.

Carol reached over Lady, walking between them, and touched Will's arm.

"I see him, Carol. FBI. Sarah's disappearance is being taken seriously."

Rick and Lorrie arrived seconds ahead of Joe Wright and Connor Murphy.

Louis got out of his car.

Dave raised his arm. "Can I have your attention, please?" His voice rasped and Carol imagined him calling Sarah's name through the remaining hours of darkness.

He waited until Louis joined him before he continued. "First, the Blue Hawks and I want to thank you again for your help. We're going to perform a grid search this morning. Experienced personnel will accompany teams of volunteers to ensure every inch of ground is covered."

As he spoke, the rising sun crested the hills behind him, flooding the landscape with light. Dave paused, raising his eyes to the cerulean blue sky.

Certainly, Carol thought, if any sign, any clue, remained to lead them to Sarah, the sun would reveal it.

Dave shook his head, took a deep breath, and placed his hand on the older man's shoulder. "Louis would like to say a few words before we begin."

"Grace is at home, praying," Louis said, his voice calm and strong. He let his gaze settle on each of them. "We need your prayers too, to help find Sarah." His hand went to a small buckskin pouch hanging from a leather cord around his neck. "We each carry a special power within ourselves. Please use yours to send her strength. I know that no matter where she is, your thoughts will keep her strong."

He insisted on shaking hands with each of them before he left to be with Grace. He even placed his hand briefly on Lady's head.

Five painstaking hours later, they had nothing.

"We've done all we can." Dave said, calling them in. His eyes were red. "You all know how special Sarah is to me, to all of us. Please don't give up on her. If you think of anything that will help us find her, call me, please."

The FBI agent stepped up to Dave and spoke a few words in his ear. Then he turned and scanned the volunteers.

Carol's breath seized when his eyes stopped on Will. The agent said something more to Dave, who shook his head. They appeared to argue. Dave finally broke away from the agent and came toward them.

"Will, can we talk?"

"Sure."

Dave flushed. "In my patrol car, Will, if you don't mind."

# 54

Carol knew why Dave wanted to talk to Will. The missing person report on Luce hadn't garnered much attention, but with Sarah missing and no sign of Luce arriving in Portland, his connection to both women made him suspect, what law enforcement called, 'a person of interest.' He wouldn't be the first man to report a missing woman when, in fact, he was responsible for her disappearance. Carol closed her eyes, thinking of Dave's sheepish face when he asked to speak with Will in private, the way the FBI agent's flat gaze followed them both on their way to Dave's car.

"Falling asleep?"

Carol started. She opened her eyes; met Will's looking down at her. "Just needed a moment. What did Dave want?"

"To ask a few questions, like where I was last night between ten and twelve."

"But you were nowhere near here."

Will rested his hand on the back of her neck. "It's routine, Carol. Dave has to be thorough. If you were missing I'd put old Joe Wright on the rack, if that meant finding you."

They walked back to his pickup, not stopping to talk with any of the others. The whole crew appeared demoralized and exhausted, each drifting off to their vehicles with barely a wave for one another.

Will remained silent until they reached Carol's. "You need to get some sleep," he said, after he cut the engine. He smoothed her hair. "I need to drive into town and let Gerry know about Sarah before the news goes public."

"Oh, God. I completely forgot about Gerry. I should go with you."

"No, I need to do this. He and Sarah were close."

"When will you be back?"

"I'm not sure."

Carol nodded. "I'll have dinner ready." She yawned, and covered her mouth with her hand. "Sorry, guess I am tired."

He walked her into the house, checked every room. He kissed the top of her head before he left. "You and Lady have a good nap."

\*\*\*

The search ended as the man knew it would, with zip, nada, nothing. Her pickup had been dusted inside and out for prints. No concern there. He never touched it. He smiled. When his onion bagel popped from the toaster, he spread it lavishly with cream cheese and took it with his coffee to the table. His good fortune the search hadn't extended far enough to encroach on the spot where he'd put Luce. But why would it? That place was well off the highway and practically buried under brush and old blackberry vines. He sipped his coffee, savoring the rich aroma. Maybe a second cup before he visits the princess and brings her up to speed on all that's being done to find her. Of course, after their last meeting, she may no longer care. He should shower again. A short nap wouldn't be amiss, either. He hadn't slept since fate delivered Sarah into his arms. He touched himself. Well, maybe a short detour before that nap.

# 55

Will looked ready to collapse. Dark half-moons bloomed under his eyes. He ate slowly, not so much from enjoyment, but because raising his arms took too much energy. He needed sleep but kept telling her he'd sleep later.

When he set his fork aside and looked up, Carol braced herself.

"I tried Luce's cell again. Her mailbox was full. Not like her to ignore that. She might not return calls but she listens to her messages." The lines around his mouth deepened. "I went to see Sheriff McReady after I spoke to Gerry. I got his okay to drive to Portland."

She nodded and set her tea down. "You meant to go earlier, before the storm. Let Gerry and me take care of the clients while you're gone. "

"You'd keep Lady with you?"

At the sound of her name, Lady whined.

"Of course."

His fingers drummed the tabletop. "Okay," he said. "I'll give Gerry a call after dinner. We'll drive to my place so I can pack for the trip. You drive the pickup back and I'll follow in my car." He frowned. "You can drive a pickup, right? Stick shift?"

"Yes. It's been a while but I haven't forgotten. "

He smiled and reached for his fork again. "We'll see. You can drive us to my place."

"Good," she said, with more confidence than she felt.

An errant breeze ruffled the crowns of the locust trees in the yard, sending a flurry of leaves past the French door. They looked like green butterflies.

Lady snored gently beneath the table. Candles flickered between the platters of chicken and mashed potatoes, the bowls of gravy and green beans, her little cast iron teapot. In spite of everything, Carol felt a wave of contentment. She would take it wherever she found it.

*** 

Will left while it was still dark. Carol wanted to make him breakfast but he shook his head. "I'll stop at the espresso place before I leave Pendleton. You have a long day ahead. Go back to bed." He kissed her and she wrapped her arms around him. "Sure you can't stay a little while longer?"

"Don't tempt me," he murmured. "I'll call you tonight."

She did lay down and to her surprise, drifted back to sleep fully clothed. When she woke an hour later, she felt snug and content. Then she remembered.

Sarah.

She let Lady outside while she filled her bowls with food and fresh water.

After oatmeal and two cups of coffee, Carol and Lady jumped into Will's pickup and headed for town.

She met Gerry at the Dalton's. Together they went over the day's work list. After he unloaded the riding mower, Carol left for her first job – the Milbank's. Will would be unhappy about her going there alone, but Milbank had no interest in her. She was too old and too ugly. She found the beer-bellied man waiting for her and thought, not for the first time, that with his florid complexion and smoker's wheeze, he was a heart attack waiting to happen. She forced a smile as she approached him.

"Won't need you anymore," he said. "I've decided to take care of the place myself."

That wasn't his real reason, Carol knew, but didn't care. She wouldn't miss him at all. But she kept her tone pleasant. "Call us if you change your mind."

At the next house, a noticeably embarrassed Virginia Boyd kept her eyes fastened on Carol's feet while she explained a friend from Winter had called to tell her about Sarah.

"I'm very sorry to hear it. She said another woman, one who lived with Will, has gone away, too." She licked her lips. "I'm sure Will hasn't done anything wrong," she mumbled, "but George...well, you know how husbands are."

Beetle-browed George made Carol glad she didn't know how husbands were. She'd seen how he treated his mousy wife, with sarcasm and contempt, a bully using words instead of fists. Once she overheard him complaining his coffee was too weak. The more his wife apologized, the worse he got. She'd hoped Virginia would tell him to make his own damn coffee or shut up, but of course that didn't happen.

She sighed with relief when she reached the third and last house on the list. No cancellation note taped to the storage shed, and no one at home. She weeded the flower beds and mowed the lawn while Lady reclined under a linden tree with her head between her paws, following every move. A couple of times Carol stopped working to stroke the dog's head and tell her what a good girl she was.

Gerry's eyebrows almost disappeared into his hairline when she got back to the Dalton's. "You can't have finished so soon. Who are you? Wonder Woman?"

She shook her head. "The rumor mill is grinding away, Gerry. Someone from Winter called the Larson's about Sarah and added that Luce was gone too. I don't know if Margaret Larson called the Milbank's, but I wouldn't be surprised."

Gerry's mouth tightened. "Screw them." His hands balled into fists. "Goddamn it. None of this seems real. You hear about terrible things, but you never think they can happen to you."

"No, you don't."

Gerry's mouth twisted. His hand flew out as though to snatch the words back. "I'm sorry. I didn't mean –"

Carol shook her head. "Don't apologize. I used to think the same thing."

# 56

Late that afternoon, Will called. The roar of background traffic nearly drowned out his voice.

"You're near the highway."

"Yeah, my motel is off I-5. How did it go today, any problems?"

"None." She refused to add to his worries. "You'll be glad to know that Gerry and I are caught up."

"I'm impressed. How many extra hours did it take to pull that off?"

"Only a couple." She lied. "How are things there?"

"Nothing, so far. The guy who claimed to see Luce was a dud, just like Dave thought."

"What about her girlfriend, Penny?"

"I talked to her. She looked a little strung out, but I believed her when she said she hadn't seen Luce."

"So when are you coming home?"

"I have an appointment in the morning with Luce's old boss and one with the kids' case worker later in the afternoon. Maybe after that. I'll call as soon as I know anything."

***

Carol was heating vegetable soup for dinner when Lorrie called.

"Come eat with us."

"But I've made soup."

"Keep it for tomorrow's lunch. We haven't had a real conversation since – gosh – before the storm."

"Lady's with me."

"I know. Will told us she's on guard duty. Bring her. She can chase around the yard with Bandit and Beau. Dogs like to socialize too, you know. Hurry now. Dinner in half an hour."

***

"I didn't realize how hungry I was." Carol folded her napkin and laid it beside her plate. "Chicken and dumplings beats soup any day. Thanks for inviting me."

"Thanks for bringing dessert. Molasses crinkles are my favorite cookie."

They took their coffee to the porch while the two boys cleared the table.

Rick leaned against the railing, leaving the porch swing to Carol and Lorrie. "No news from Will, I take it."

They had avoided talk of Sarah or Luce while at the table, letting the boys entertain them with stories from school.

No," Carol said. "He's staying the night, and will talk to Luce's old boss in the morning." She almost added, 'and the children's case worker,' but stopped herself. She didn't know how much Rick and Lorrie knew about Luce's background.

"You know," Lorrie said, "I wasn't worried about Luce, even when Will didn't hear from her. I was mad. After all he did for her, she didn't say goodbye, or thanks for the free ride." Lorrie shook her head. "Now, with Sarah missing, I don't know what to think." She pushed against the floorboards with her feet, setting the swing in motion. Minutes passed without conversation, and Carol supposed that each of them were thinking the same thing – what had become of Sarah and Luce, how were Dave and the Blue Hawks holding up?

Lorrie was the first to break their silence. "You haven't mentioned Malone. Shouldn't his trial be coming up soon?"

Carol swallowed the last of her coffee and set the mug on an upturned apple box standing beside the swing. "He has a preliminary hearing next week. He pled not guilty at his arraignment. Apparently, he's waiving a jury trial and letting the judge decide his case."

"He can do that?"

"Sure." Carol knew she sounded bitter but didn't care. "He'll count on his charm and his professional standing to get him off." She hooked her hands together, felt her nails bite into skin. "He'll admit to having a few beers, looking up an old girlfriend and before he knew it, her new boyfriend sicced his dog on him."

"That's nuts," Lorrie said.

"Yes." Carol opened her hands and flexed her fingers. "Dave found another woman in Tom's past, one who's still too afraid of him to show for the hearing. I'm hoping her deposition will be allowed."

Lorrie dragged her feet, stopping the swing's motion. "Whoa. What woman? What deposition?"

"Will didn't tell you?"

"No, he didn't." Lorrie said. "Rick, have you been holding out on me?"

"You know better, sweets. Too much going on of late. None of us have had much time for talk."

Lorrie turned back to Carol. "Okay. Start at the beginning, please."

"Dave checked further into Tom's background and found another victim."

Rick gave a low whistle. "A real lady's man, this guy."

"She didn't file a police report," Carol said. "But a co-worker told their department head what happened. He let Tom go." Carol swallowed, old hurt welling inside. "Unlike the dean, who accused me of slandering a wonderful teacher, her boss stood up for her."

"Malone really put you through it, didn't he?" Rick said.

"No, what the dean and my co-workers put me through was much worse. They took his word over mine." She bit her lip.

"Well, I bet they're feeling pretty damn stupid now," Lorrie offered, "and even if that woman's deposition can't be used, I refuse to believe a judge would fall for Malone's line of bull. If he does, I'll know the world really has gone mad." She got to her feet and pulled Carol up with her. "Let's go for a walk. The dogs need exercising." She motioned to Rick. "Do you want to join us, honey?"

"Nope. I'll leave you ladies to it. I'm going to shoot hoops with the boys if they're done with those dishes." He patted his flat stomach and smiled. "Gotta stay in shape, you know."

He leaned over and kissed Lorrie's cheek, then Carol's. "See you two later."

\*\*\*

"You're a lucky woman," Carol said when they left on their walk, the three dogs dancing around their legs.

"I swear, sometimes it scares me, knowing just how lucky," Lorrie said. "Especially now." A rueful smile played on her lips. "I find myself wondering about men I've known for years. I see them and think, where were you when Luce and Sarah vanished? I hate that."

Carol stooped, picked up a downed cottonwood branch, and threw it for the dogs. All three scrambled after it. "Will lost two clients today. People ready to believe guilt by association. I didn't tell him when he called."

Bandit, one of the two Heelers, returned triumphant, stick clutched between his jaws, his blue mottled coat dappled with bits brush. He dropped it at Lorrie's feet, quivering with anticipation.

"Good boy," Lorrie praised. She patted his head before she let the branch fly again.

For a while they were content to walk, stopping to congratulate whichever dog returned with the prize. They were like well-behaved children, taking turns retrieving, never fighting over it.

Pine, alder, and cottonwood lined both sides of the road; the cottonwood leaves flashing in the errant breeze. Off to their right, the Umatilla made its way west, a sound like a low, steady wind. Hard to believe anything bad could happen in a place so beautiful, but Sarah had disappeared just a few miles from here, perhaps Luce as well.

"Careful." Lorrie grabbed Carol's arm and pulled her further onto the shoulder as a battered blue and white Chevy pickup came around the bend.

Joe Wright slowed, tooted his horn and waved a greeting.

"Going to check on his hives, I bet." she said, returning his wave. She looked at her watch. "We should probably turn back. Maybe someone has called with news."

But when they reached the house, Rick, shooting baskets with the boys, gave a small shake of his head.

"I'm going inside to check the answering machine," Lorrie said.

Carol followed her in. Lorrie's thoughts mirrored her own. If Sarah wasn't found soon, the unthinkable would become true.

# 57

Carol drove home in the dark. She changed into a cotton robe, put on slipper sox, and curled up on the sofa with Tana French's *Back Harbor*. Maybe not the best kind of read at a time like this, but she was a diehard French fan. Lady stretched out on the floor nearby.

After the first few pages, she closed the book. She couldn't recall a single word. Too many thoughts ricocheting through her brain: Will, and his search for Luce, Sarah's disappearance, the specter of facing Malone at his hearing. She'd been surprised he decided against a jury trial. She'd have thought he'd enjoy playing to a jury, enjoy her humiliation when she was forced to answer questions, questions like: When did you become intimate? If you thought this man so dangerous, why did you sleep with him? Why did you give him a key to your apartment?

Even now, her stupidity shamed her. Why had it taken so long to realize the face he showed the world was false?

She'd been a loner most of her life. You couldn't lose what you didn't have, she used to think, and relationships were tricky things. She had her apartment, and a job she loved. Easy banter with coworkers substituted for a social life. At the end of the day, she looked forward to returning to her quiet rooms, a glass of wine, a Miles Davis or Ramsey Lewis CD on the player while she prepared dinner. Weekends she treated herself to cappuccino and pastry at her favorite patisserie, shopped at the Farmers' Market, and when in the mood, went to the movies. A more than satisfactory existence, she believed, a contented one, and if there were moments – a loving look shared by a couple, a sleeping baby cuddled against its father's chest, laughter shared by a family at the table next to her – that caused her to think otherwise, she refused to acknowledge them. Until Tom Malone entered her life. She, who never considered herself lonely, discovered she'd been living a lie. Fresh flowers, delivered to her door. Gifts – small, funny ones at first, like the bag of fortune cookies he left on her desk; later, a hand-painted box with a delicate necklace inside – a single pearl on an intricate gold chain. He took her to dinner in exclusive restaurants, ordered expensive wines, told her how beautiful she was, how smart.

Carol jumped at Lady's sharp bark, spilling her book to the floor. She glanced at the clock. "I'm sorry, girl. It's time, isn't it?" She retrieved the book and set it on the coffee table before she got up to let her outside.

While Lady did her business Carol waited on the porch, admiring the star-thick sky, the fragrant perfume of pine and grass. The pods on the cottonwoods were opening and ghostly puffs of white floated through the yard light's yellow glow. Uncle

James used to say when the cottonwood flew, it meant the salmon were coming home.

She had been eight that summer, the first of many spent in Winter. He had taken her to the creek to watch for the salmon, pointed them out where they swam or rested in shaded pools beneath boulders or cottonwood roots. Later, they watched them spawn. Their dying afterwards had come as a shock to her eight-year-old self, and when James tried to explain this was the natural order of things, she had covered her ears and run from the room.

Lady leaped back onto the porch and butted Carol with her head.

"Good girl," Carol said. "Now let's go to bed."

Before she got under the covers, Carol sent her most positive thoughts for Sarah's safety and Will's success in finding Luce.

Sleep came quickly but she bolted awake within the hour, gasping for air like a swimmer too long underwater. She threw her legs over the side of the bed and pressed her hands to her chest, trying to slow her racing heart, trying to erase the images from her nightmare: a forest where fish instead of leaves hung from the trees, gills fluttering in their desperate fight to breathe. Sarah, eyes pleading, her locket held open to reveal not her son Brandon, but a dazed little girl whom Carol instinctively recognized as Luce as she looked when rescued from the fraternity house.

She stumbled to the bathroom and bathed her face with cold water. She couldn't chase the images away, not even when she climbed back into bed and Lady jumped up and stretched out beside her. "Only a bad dream, girl," Carol murmured, as she stroked Lady's warm back. "Only a bad dream."

# 58

He pours Lily of the Valley bath salts into the running water and watches the tub fill with foam. When the bubbles near the rim, he turns off the taps and returns to the bedroom. She looks no bigger than a child against the blood-spattered plastic. This bothers him. Though he enjoyed every moment with her while he was *in* the moment, he feels his elation ebb. This has never happened before. Ever. He leans down and runs his fingers through her blue-black hair, a color no dye can duplicate. He slides his arms beneath her, forming a cradle, and lifts and carries her to the bath.

Pearly bubbles shade pink to crimson when he lowers her in. He uses a thick sponge around the bite marks, the cuts from the fillet knife that opened her flesh. How pale she is now that the blood beneath her copper skin is still. He drains and refills the tub twice more until the water runs clear. She slumps against the white enamel of the tub while he reaches for the bleach.

He rolls up the stained plastic sheet and covers the mattress with a new one. Over this he spreads a blue nylon blanket with blue satin binding. A popular department store brand sold by the thousands. He centers her body on this and takes a brush to her midnight hair, dipping his face close to its silkiness, inhaling the last of her. Pausing from his work, he raises the blind and looks out into the moonlit dark where the ragged silhouettes of pines stand like sentinels against the sky. Perfect. He closes the blind and returns to Sarah.

She is unbelievably light when he carries her from the room, out of the house and into the trees. He moves with confidence. His feet know the way. A scream shatters the silence, abruptly dies. He freezes, pulse ratcheting. When the air above him vibrates, he expels his breath. An owl with its kill, a rabbit, he thinks, identifying the scream. He moves on. A few minutes more and he will reach the house, a ruinous shell almost invisible under its coating of vines and old growth, filled with crawling things and years of debris. At twilight bats pour like smoke from the crumbling chimney. He places Sarah's body under a thorn tree while he clears brush and barbed wire from the door. When he's done, he stands in the open frame, his breathing shallow while he adjusts to the odor that hangs inside like polluted fog and clogs the back of his throat.

He carries Sarah over the threshold like a bride, lowers her gently to the floor of what was once a bedroom. He strikes a match, holds the flame to the blackened wicks of cheap white candles fastened by their own melted wax to cast-off containers: a tuna can, a cracked saucer with a border of flowers, a green wine bottle with a faded label. The odor is overpowering and he takes a large handkerchief from his pocket and wraps it bandit-style over his nose and mouth. Flickering light sends eerie shadows dancing across the walls and ceiling. Red eyes spark from a corner, disappear. Something rat-sized skitters past him.

Plastic gloves for his hands. A Swiss army knife to cut the twine. He loosens the blanket, exposing Sarah's neck, hands and breasts. He fans out her hair, forming a dark halo around her head. She resembles a fourteenth century Madonna, her bloodless face like polished bronze, her wounds those of a martyr's. Her eyes gleam as they stare blindly through the ruined roof to the stars beyond. Not an unpleasant way to spend eternity, he thinks, though he knows her eyes will be the first to go once the crows and rats discover her. His groin tightens. He wants to touch all her secret places again, wants to run his tongue the length of her, over the bruised flesh and indentations, want to push it into the knife cuts that resemble silent screams. He forces saliva into his mouth. He must swallow his need. She is cleansed. Rigor is setting in. He blows out the candles.

Outside, he removes his handkerchief and sucks in grateful breaths of night air. He reviews every step he's taken while he rearranges brush and barbed wire over the door. Finally, he removes his gloves, puts them with the handkerchief into a back pocket, and starts for home. He hasn't gone more than a few yards when he hears rustling and a dark figure appears on the path ahead. His heart punches a hole in his chest. Then it's gone, crashing through the brush. A deer. Spooked by a goddamn deer!

# 59

L ate afternoon sunlight shimmered over the landscape, coating it in gold. Carol sat on the porch, sipping tea. She'd used the mower again and the lawn was an even blanket of green. The phone lay beside her, ready for Will's call. Lady sprawled nearby.

The deer were back, grazing quietly in the far corner near a young pine. If she could describe their delicate grace in words, she'd have a perfect haiku.

The phone rang. The deer bolted.

"Will?"

"Hi, Carol. Has there been any word on Sarah?"

"No."

"Damn. I hoped by now..."

"Where are you?" She hoped he might be calling from the road.

"In Portland. I'm staying another day. I met with the social worker this afternoon. Luce never contacted her."

"So why are you staying on?"

"I have permission to visit the children, but that can't be arranged until tomorrow afternoon. I'll do some shopping in the morning, buy the kids some toys. I'll tell them they're from their mother."

Carol wondered how much the children understood of their mother's absence. They were so young. The loss of her over the last four months, and their placement with another family had to be confusing, if not traumatic.

"Carol?"

"I'm sorry, what did you say?"

"I asked if work went okay today."

"Yes, it did. We're caught up now and able to stick with our three-day weekend."

"How's my dog?"

"Snoozing at my feet. Do you want to talk to her?"

"I'll pass," he said with a soft laugh. "Just don't spoil her too much. I'll check in again tomorrow evening."

"I'll be here."

"That's the thought that keeps me going," Will said, and hung up before she could answer.

\*\*\*

The following morning, Carol ticked off her mental list. Her little vegetable garden needed weeding, the kitchen and bathroom floors needed mopping, and everything else could stand a once over with a dust rag and vacuum cleaner. She was considering where to begin when the phone shrilled.

Too soon for Will. Lorrie, maybe?

She picked up. "Hello."

"Carol, Deputy Ron Baldwin. It looks like Malone skipped town."

"What? But the preliminary hearing is next week."

"His lady friend called the city police early this morning. Says he took her car last night to go to the drugstore and never came back. The car isn't all that's missing. The cash in her purse is gone too."

"What happens now?"

"The lady is spitting mad. She's filed a stolen car report."

"But where do you think Tom went?"

"If I were Tom," Baldwin said, "I'd drive to Portland, ditch the car in long term parking and take a flight to parts unknown."

Carol turned the possibilities around in her mind. Tom could have made the Portland Airport by nine, taken a late a flight to Sacramento and ridden the shuttle to his apartment in Fairfield for his passport.

She brought her attention back to Baldwin.

"... keep you posted, Carol. But honestly, I think with the head start he got, we're unlikely to find him. He'd be a fool to show his face here again."

"So the hearing is cancelled."

"No." Baldwin cleared his throat. "Malone could change his mind and come back, but he'd have a lot of explaining to do.

Maybe he could even talk his lady friend into dropping her charges, but frankly, I don't see any of that happening. I think he's gone for good. I'll let you know if I learn anything more."

After she hung up, Carol tried to comprehend what she'd been told. Was she really free of Tom after all this time? She wanted to believe that. She didn't care that he might never be caught, might never spend time in jail for what he'd done. Let him be the one to run for a change, let him know what it was like to be hunted, to lose what he valued most – his livelihood, his reputation, his freedom to go where he wanted, when he wanted.

Too much was happening too fast. She couldn't process it all. She had to get out of the house.

She snapped her fingers for Lady.

# 60

L ady loped alongside Carol. They reached the highway, crossed to the other side, and crawled under a barbed wire fence into the meadow. A well-worn path led them past Joe Wright's bee hives and into a wooded area of fir, alder and cottonwood bordering the river. They were in the deepest part of the woods when Lady came to an abrupt stop. She raised her muzzle, testing the air. Her good ear flattened against her skull. A low, menacing growl rumbled up through her chest and into her throat. Carol knew cougar and bear roamed the canyon but rarely left the safety of the ridge at this time of day. "What's wrong, girl?" Lady's hackles had risen like porcupine quills. Her growl became an ululating howl. Carol felt a cold tickle on the back of her neck, an icy finger that made its way down her spine. She didn't know whether to backtrack the way they'd come or stay where she was until some sign from Lady. The dog made the decision for both of them. She leaped from the path and raced off, mindless of brush and thorn trees.

Carol plunged after her, using her arms to ward off brambles and branches. A low-hanging alder limb caught her, burning a path from hairline to jaw. A slick of blood came away on her palm when she wiped her face. She ignored it and pushed on, drawn by Lady's eerie howls. A cacophony of harsh cries erupted as an explosion of black wings flapped above the tree line. Crows. Dozens of them. But where had they come from? And why were they so angry? Lady's howls were subsiding into shrill, insistent barks that scraped Carol's nerve endings raw. She forged ahead, skirted a mountain of blackberry vine, and stopped again, disoriented. She hadn't realized how turned around she was. Lady had led her to a long-abandoned house, one she remembered from childhood, a ruin even then, and a place her uncle insisted she steer clear of. "It's filled with black widows and bats and god knows what else," he'd said, 'not to mention the floor is rotting, you could fall through."

She saw a gaping hole in the roof. Cinderblocks had crumbled away from the chimney and lay covered in moss, half buried by weeds. A flutter of wings forced her eyes up again. The crows were settling on branches of cottonwood. Their silence spooked her. They appeared to be waiting, but for what? Lady keened from inside the house. Carol clenched her fists and willed herself forward. A twisted mass of brush and rusted barbed wire blocked the doorway. She didn't bother trying to free it, and searched for an empty window frame instead. She found one, eased herself over the sill, and tested the floor inside with one foot before putting all her weight onto the rotten boards. Behind a door wedged shut with a plank of wood, Lady whimpered, which meant she had found another way inside. Carol skirted a soggy mattress, empty bottles, and rat droppings. She stubbed her toe on a curling edge of rotten linoleum, lost her balance, but righted herself before she fell. Lady's barks came in short, excited bursts now.

Carol struggled with the plank blocking the door, lost her grip, and cried out as a sliver lodged deep in her palm. Holding back a scream, she pulled it free. She wiped her hand on her jeans and grabbed the knob. The door refused to budge. Almost crying with frustration, Carol turned the knob as far as it would go and kicked the bottom panel with all her strength. With a crack like a gunshot, the door shuddered open.

The smell rocked her back on her heels, closed her throat and burned her eyes. An angry whine filled the room, and in the dim light a dense black cloud rose from the floor and circled the gaping hole in the ceiling. The air thickened and swelled, pressing against her eardrums until she thought they might burst. Flies. Thousands of flies, interrupted from... Carol gagged and doubled over. "Lady, come girl, come away," she croaked. Lady trembled but stood her ground. The explosion of crows, the flies... Carol tasted bile, swallowed hard and forced herself closer to what lay bundled on the floor. A spill of blue-black hair, peacock feathers in folded hands, empty eye sockets fixed on the bit of sky visible through the ruined roof, a cowry shell earring glinting in one ear. "Sarah," Carol whispered.

She was dimly aware of candles – all white – placed near Sarah's body in a variety of containers. The flies were returning, humming with activity, settling. Carol bit on her lip until she tasted blood.

Sarah was not alone. The face was gone, the flesh ripped and torn, exposing bone. A dream catcher earring lay in the hollow between head and shoulder. Luce's blonde hair was dull and matted, and bald spots gleamed where tufts had been ripped from the skull. A stub of candle sat in a small dish bordered with flowers. How many nests had the birds made from her hair? Stomach roiling, Carol backed away. She had to get help. She had to call the sheriff. Oh, dear God. Dave! "Lady, come." Lady whined but didn't move. "Okay, girl, I understand. Protect them. I'll be back." Jackson was closest. Carol hoped he was home. She ran breathing in sobs, images of ravaged flesh torturing her vision. One minute she was in motion, the next slamming into a rock hard chest. A scream clawed its way up her throat.

# 61

"Yes, that's right," Carol said. "The abandoned house near the river. Will's dog, Lady, is with the bodies. I'll meet you there." She took in a deep breath. "Sheriff McReady? Please don't let Dave come, I'd hate for him to... yes," she whispered. "Thank you."

Still holding the phone, she turned to Jackson.

"I heard," he said. "I'm coming with you."

She nodded, relieved to hear him speak. He hadn't said a word since she stumbled into him and described the scene that lay behind her. He had wrapped his massive arms around her and kept them there all the way to his house. Inside, he made her drink hot tea, and when she stopped shaking, dialed the sheriff and handed her the phone.

Now she needed to call Will. She dreaded what she had to tell him, but couldn't imagine asking anyone else to deliver the news. While she waited for him to answer, she sneaked another look at Jackson. This latest shock had carved even deeper grooves in his face. Will had told her how the big man blamed himself for not seeing Luce home on the day she attempted to leave Winter. Now, with no doubt as to what became of her – and of Sarah – he was taking on another layer of guilt, thinking if only he'd stuck with Luce that day, this might not have happened. Carol had a flash of memory, his beaming face the night he waltzed Luce under the stars. She jerked back to the present when Will's voice mail answered. She handed the phone back to Jackson. She couldn't leave a message for this kind of news. "He's not answering, Jackson. We'd better go."

On their way to the door she noticed the vase filled with peacock feathers on the credenza beside Jackson's CD player.

She hesitated, a new chill sweeping over her. Those feathers. They popped up everywhere, it seemed. On the roadside, in Ben's parking lot, on bodies...

Jackson, at the door, held out his hand. "Are you sure you can do this?"

"I have to," Carol said. Ignoring his outstretched hand, she walked out ahead of him.

\*\*\*

Hold on, Carol told herself, repeating the words like a mantra. And hold on she did. She held on while standing outside the house, calling Lady. She held on when the team of strangers arrived to examine the scene, and when they carried what remained of Sarah and Luce out in zippered body bags.

Jackson stayed by her side, a monolith carved from stone. When the sheriff finished interviewing her, Jackson insisted on accompanying her home, and stayed with her, heating soup and brewing tea that he loaded with sugar, insisting she needed nourishment to stay on her feet.

Will, contacted by the sheriff's office, made it home in record time. She remembered his look of anguish when he came through the door, the way his arms wrapped around her in a bone-crushing embrace, but after that, time blurred. She vaguely recalled Jackson leaving, Sheriff McReady coming to interview her a second time, Lorrie holding her hand when Will left her to call Gerry with the terrible news.

Awake or asleep, she remained haunted by what she had found in that rotting house; haunted too, by a tenuous image fragile as old lace that teased her mind but dissolved when she tried bringing it into focus. She didn't mention it to anyone because she had no way to explain it, but it nagged at her, the way a melody sometimes did, familiar, but impossible to name.

***

Another week passed. The medical examiner released the bodies and Will and the Blue Hawks moved forward with funerals.

Sarah was going home to Montana for burial. Louis and Grace held services in their home the evening before the trip. Carol had found a measure of comfort in the drumming and singing, but Dave sat grim-faced through the ceremony, fists clenched on his knees, his eyes hard as stone. The Dave she knew was gone. She wondered if he would ever return.

Under a June sky marbled with lucent clouds, Rick and Lorrie, Ben, Jackson, the Murphy family, and the Wrights gathered in the cemetery with Will and Carol. Tribal police had volunteered to stand guard, keeping the curious and the media from disturbing the burial.

Will spoke of Luce's battle with life; the death of her parents when she was twelve, her fight to survive as a throwaway child living on the streets of Portland. He talked about her wry sense of humor, her friendship with his mother. He praised her strength. "Luce never had it easy, but she never gave up. She was a good mother, who had to leave her children for awhile until she could conquer an addiction that came from being hospitalized. Her two sons meant everything to her and getting back to them was the most important thing on her mind." When he mentioned her children, a low moan came from Lureen Wright.

His request to let the children attend had been denied.

"Too traumatic, they barely remember her, anyway," said their caseworker. "Why upset them?"

Fresh flowers blanketed Luce's grave. Miniature pink roses in terra cotta pots, white lilies nestled in green ferns, verbena, and long-stemmed yellow roses for remembrance. The florist in Pendleton had been kept busy. Many in the canyon also brought bouquets of wildflowers mixed with branches of pine.

After everyone left, Carol remained with Will at the foot of the grave. She could only guess what thoughts ran through his mind; grief, anger, and worst of all, guilt, because he had not succeeded in keeping her safe. She slipped her hand through his. He squeezed back so tight she winced.

"I was so Goddamn angry at her for repeating the same dumb mistakes again and again."

She pressed against his side. "You did everything you could."

"I wish I could believe that." He bent to smooth earth dislodged by the weight of the flowers. When he straightened he said, "Luce and Sarah died because they trusted a familiar face. Wondering who that face belongs to is going to tear this canyon apart."

# 62

The man sits on the bed staring out the window. The view usually calms him but this morning his mind is restless, conflicted.

He feels bad about Carol finding the bodies, though he expected someone would, sooner or later. Had she noticed his one little slip? It didn't seem so. He would have read the knowledge in her eyes. He believes he's hidden his past well, but one can never be sure. He hates the idea of disappearing, starting over again somewhere else, but it wouldn't be the first time he found it necessary to reinvent himself. He loves Winter. Yet staying might be too risky. Unless he deals with Carol. He's never killed a woman who didn't deserve to die. He doesn't think he can. He's no monster, killing without reason. This room, where Luce and Sarah died, calls to him through the night. He wakes, impelled to visit it, to lie on the bare mattress where they twisted and turned beneath him. He moans as they did, and when he comes, his cries are choked, just like their muffled screams.

What will they say of me after I'm gone? What will they write when my treasures are found? Psychiatrists and psychobabble, so many talking heads, explaining what drove me to kill: a mother who picked up strangers; the tragic loss of a little brother; the foster homes. Oh, yes, a life reduced to catch phrases voiced in somber tones: why I didn't bury my victims, why I wrapped them in blue, kept their earrings and clothing.

The peacock feathers should keep them busy. I never could resist irony. He chuckles. Such thoughts. His death is years away. Of course, there's always the chance of getting caught.

He leaves the bed and walks to a framed clipping on the wall. He stares at it for a long moment before he traces a line of text with his index finger.

I'll never get caught. I'm too smart, and I still have work to do.

# 63

Ugly whispers circulated. Every male over the age of sixteen became suspect while the investigation continued. Police canvassed and re-canvassed the canyon from the point where Sarah left Dave to the off-the-road camp of suspected drug dealers between Carol and Lorrie's. A search of the camp resulted in several arrests for drug possession, but no sign that Luce or Sarah had been held there. Families without dogs adopted them, deer hunting rifles sat within easy reach, and those who swore never to keep guns in the house went out and purchased them.

Ben complained of unwanted visitors to the store. "The kind who hope for nothing better than an old-fashioned lynching, and aren't particular about who swings at the end of the rope."

The curious came from surrounding areas, Pendleton, Milton-Freewater, Athena, Weston, Walla Walla, drawn by the sensational news coverage, stopping at Ben's in hopes of some gruesome tidbit to carry back to family and friends. Reporters from Portland and Seattle showed up as well, asking questions, snapping photos. One found himself bodily lifted by Jackson and deposited in a roadside ditch when he stuck a microphone in front of Lureen and refused to back off when Joe asked him to leave her alone.

Two days after Luce's funeral, Carol drove to the store and found the parking lot filled with vehicles, none of them familiar. Inside, she dodged a cluster of men to grab a loaf of bread. When she reached the counter Ben smiled, but the smile didn't reach his eyes.

She started to speak, but his gaze went over her shoulder to the strangers gathered in his store. His lip curled. "The media titillates them with half-truths and they come here to feed their curiosity. I've had a bellyful of them. Yesterday, a guy asked me if I knew Will Jacobs, the man who killed 'those women.'" His eyes returned to her. "I messed up his pretty cowboy hat when I showed him to the door. He thanked me with some choice words."

"Not everyone," a grating voice said behind Carol, "thinks your friend is innocent."

Carol whirled to confront a stubble faced man with chest hair curling above the neck of a dingy T-shirt spotted with grease, and a body odor so sour she had to hold her breath.

She recognized him, not by name, but by sight. She'd followed behind his pickup a time or two on her way to Pendleton. Stickers on the bumper and rear window: 'If it has titties or wheels expect trouble,' 'Cowboys do it in the saddle,' 'Cowgirls use spurs.'

Forty going on fifteen, she'd concluded.

Apparently aware of her disgust, he thrust his face closer.

She thought of kneeing him in the groin.

The tip of his tongue flicked out, a snake, ready to strike. "Seen you with him, lady. I'd look out, I was you, or you might end up like they did."

"Out!" Ben said. The force of his rage sizzled through the room like a downed power line. It cleared the store. Even the open-jawed onlookers scuttled out.

"Don't pay any attention to that creep," Ben said. "Man lives in a broken down trailer with holes in the roof and weeds poking up through the floor and hasn't done an honest day's work since I came here. Ask me, that's who the police should be looking at."

"When will it end, Ben?"

"When a bigger tragedy strikes." He patted her hand. "Hang in there, Carol. And come by some morning for coffee. We haven't done that in a long time."

"I'd like that."

When Carol stepped off the porch into the parking lot, she noticed three of the strangers from the store standing beside a green SUV. They made no attempt to disguise their interest in her. One muttered a few words under his breath. Carol caught the word, 'scar face,' before laughter erupted from all three. She got into the car, started the engine, and reversed so fast that they had to jump out of the way or risk being hit. She stomped on the gas and drove off in a spray of gravel, seeing the raised middle finger of one man in her rear view mirror. "Who's laughing now, you bastards?" she said, feeling better than she had in days.

\*\*\*

Carol glanced at the clock. Will must be crossing the bridge because Lady stood at the door, head canted. Amazing, how animals sensed things. She emptied the dregs of her tea into the sink.

Five minutes later, Will came through the door, kneeled beside an ecstatic Lady, and scratched along her back and behind her ears, crooning nonsensical love words.

"I think I'm jealous," Carol said.

"No need," he said. "You're both my best girls." He got to his feet and enveloped her in a tight embrace.

"Are you going to scratch behind my ears, too?"

Will released her with a light slap on her bottom. "Not until I get something cold to drink."

"How'd work go today?" she asked, when he returned with a cold beer and joined her on the sofa.

"At least no one else quit on me." He took a long swallow and blew out a sigh. "This hits the spot." He took another drink, balanced the glass on his knee and rolled it between his hands. "I guess Milbank couldn't think of anyone else to call."

Will and Gerry saw to the remaining clients. At present, there wasn't enough work to include Carol. She had been more relieved than disappointed when Will broke the news. Returning to places she and Sarah worked together was more than she could handle, at least for now.

Wilma, sweet, thoughtful Wilma, continued to send foil-wrapped crumb cake home with Will every Monday. They had driven there to tell her about Sarah, not wanting her to hear the news elsewhere. "Stay in touch, dear, please," she had said, gripping Carol's hand. "I don't want to lose you too."

Will finished his beer and stood. "How about a quick walk before I head home?"

"You're on."

\*\*\*

Quail chattered in the brush. Wild rose and blackberry blossoms lent a subtle sweetness to the air. Lady ran circles around trees, barked at minnows, and snuffled through the brush teasing birds.

"Lady's enjoying herself."

"Yes." Carol chose her next words carefully. "Lorrie and I are going to Walla Walla tomorrow. You should take Lady to town with you. She'd enjoy that much more than staying inside the house all day."

Will stopped, a frown creasing his forehead. "What time are you leaving?"

"A little after eight. We don't expect to get home before three. You'll be back by then, and if you're not, Lorrie will stay until you are."

He placed his hands on either side of her face, his gaze searching. "Promise?"

"Promise."

# 64

"Your best girl is raring to go," Carol said.

"She'll have to be patient," Will said, swallowing the last of his orange juice. "We stay until Lorrie gets here."

"Don't be silly, Will. She'll be here in the next half hour."

"I'm not being silly. And why are you going this early? The stores don't open for another three hours."

"We're going to have breakfast at that restaurant in Walla Walla, the one Ben said serves corned beef hash and eggs."

Looking at the stubborn set of his jaw, Carol had to smile. "I'll stay inside with the door locked until she comes."

Will tousled her hair before he pushed back from the table. "Okay, boss. We'll go. Now walk us out. I want to hear the bolt slide in place once I'm on the other side of that door."

Lady, hearing chairs scrape, slipped from her spot under the table, ear perked. When Will opened the door and motioned her outside instead of telling her to stay, she looked from him to Carol, and back again, puzzled.

"Go girl, you get to keep him company today."

She shot the bolt after they left. Will rapped in response. She had to laugh, watching the two on their way to the pickup. Will walked, but Lady bounced so high off the ground she looked airborne. When they reached the gate, Will turned and waved. Before he could open it, Lady dropped to her belly, scooted underneath, and raced to the driver's door where she stood quivering, waiting for him to let her inside.

After they drove away, Carol gathered her purse, jacket and sunglasses and placed them on the sofa, ready to grab when Lorrie arrived. She hadn't realized how much this outing meant to her until now. Escape, if only for a few hours, from the sadness and fear that held the canyon hostage.

The phone rang as she finished putting on lipstick

"Mike's been throwing up since four this morning," Lorrie said. "Now he says his stomach hurts 'really bad.' Afraid we're on our way to the hospital. Sorry about our plans."

"I'll come to the hospital with you."

"Thanks, but Rick is driving us, and little brother is coming too. I think he's enjoying Mike's pain a bit too much, the brat. I'll call you as soon as we know anything."

Carol hung up. Now what? She had cleaned every inch of the house inside, mowed the lawn, and weeded the garden beds. She had fought her nightmares by staying busy. Trouble was, she'd busied herself out of anything to do.

She thought about visiting Dave, back from Montana, but still on leave from work. Will had stopped to see him but said the visit had not gone well.

"Dave looks like hell," he had said. "And he didn't want company. He asked me to leave."

No. she wouldn't trespass on Dave's privacy. All she could do, all any of them could do, was wait until he was ready to let them back into his life.

Should she call Will, tell him Lorrie cancelled?

He'd worry. Worse, he'd insist on bringing Lady back which would make him late for work. He couldn't afford to lose any more business. She glanced at the clock. Rick and Lorrie's drive to the hospital would take about forty minutes. They'd spend another hour waiting while tests were run.

She thought of Ben's recent invitation to coffee. She could bike to the store within ten minutes, and enjoy a short visit with him. An hour, no more; back in plenty of time for Lorrie's call. She'd confess to Will later.

# 65

Will sat alone in the emergency room lounge tapping his foot, wondering what else could go wrong. On a television bolted to the wall, a smiling blonde in a lime-green took a seat behind a crescent-shaped news desk. Her mouth moved in a parody of sound. He had grown tired of the noise and turned off the volume.

"Will? What in hell are you doing here?"

Surprised, Will looked up into Rick's unshaven face. Thirteen-year-old Robbie stood at his side, his copper hair, unruly as his mother's, freshly tamed with water.

"Damn, Robbie. I swear you've grown another foot in the last two weeks. What are your parents feeding you kids, anyway?"

Robbie flushed with pleasure. "Dad says I'm havin' a 'spurt.'"

Will turned back to Rick. "Gerry was splicing a length of hose and the knife slipped." Will frowned. "What brings you two here?"

"Mike. Stomach ache. When he started throwing up Lorrie thought he might have appendicitis, so we came barreling into town." Rick rubbed his hand against the stubble on his jaw. "Didn't even get to shave." He winked at Robbie. "Sorta manly, though, don't you think? Makes me look rugged, like Bruce Willis, maybe Robert Downey?"

Robbie rolled his eyes.

Rick mimed hurt. "No respect. I get no respect from anyone in this family."

"So, is Mike okay?" Will asked.

"He's fine. Doc says simple indigestion." Rick shook his head and elbowed Robbie. "Damn kids, more trouble than they're worth. Don't know why we ever had them."

"This from the guy who snorted a Red Hot up his nose and screamed like a baby."

Robbie perked up. "Huh?"

"Never you mind, son," Rick said.

But Rick's growing grin said he remembered the incident well.

"A Red Hot is a red cinnamon candy," Will explained. "When we were kids your Dad stuck one in his nose trying to be funny. Wanted me to admire his red booger. He laughed so hard at his own joke, he snorted it up where he couldn't get it out. You should have seen him, Robbie, hopping up and down when it started to melt. 'Ow, ow, it burns, it burns.'"

"Goddam, but Mom was mad." Rick said. "After you left I told her it was your fault because you dared me."

"You dirty dog! No wonder she wouldn't talk to me for a week."

Robbie's eyes danced. "Does Mom know?"

"Forget it, kid," Rick warned. "She knows. No blackmail in it for you. In fact −" He broke off as Gerry came through the emergency room door, injured hand held at chest level.

Recognizing Rick, his eyebrows shot up. "What's going on?"

"Hey, Gerry." Rick started to offer his hand, thought better of it. "Sorry about your accident."

A metal splint encased Gerry's hand. His injured finger was mummified by gauze. "I had to get a tetanus shot, too." He shuddered. "I really hate needles."

Will rose from his chair. "I better get this guy home. Remind Carol she stays with you folks until I get back from work, will you?"

Rick shook his head. "Carol's not here. She offered to come but Lorrie told her it wasn't necessary."

"Damn, that means she's alone. I brought Lady into town with me." Will patted the cell phone in his pocket. "I'll give her a call, let her know Mike's okay." And make damn sure she's inside with the doors locked, he finished silently.

The minute the hospital doors hissed shut behind them, Will motioned Gerry to the pickup and reached for his phone.

Six rings and her voice mail came on. He made it brief: "Ran into Rick at the hospital. Mike's fine but Gerry cut his hand and needed stitches." He paused, tapping the edge of his phone with two fingers. "I'm guessing you're in the shower and can't hear the phone since you promised – I'm underlining that word promised – to stay inside. Call me when you get this."

He put the phone back in his pocket, only a little annoyed. After all she'd been through these last few months, he was damn sure she wouldn't take any chances.

Damn sure.

So why this sudden uneasiness?

# 66

Carol's excursion to Ben's took longer than she anticipated. First, her bike tires needed air. She took care of that and started out, getting as far as the mailbox before she remembered the CD she meant to take to him. She pedaled back to the house, grabbed it and set off again, only to arrive at the store to find the *Closed* sign on the door.

Damn!

About to return home, she heard music coming from the back yard. Leaning her bike against the porch steps, she followed the narrow walk around the building and found Ben on a ladder, his back to her, cutting a dead limb from a locust tree. He turned slightly, started at sight of her, and lost his balance. What happened next couldn't have taken more than a minute, but to Carol, unable to move, seemed to take place in mind-numbing slow motion. The pruning saw dropped from his hand. He tried to regain his footing and failed. Ben fell, taking the ladder down with him, striking his forehead. Before she could move toward him, he sat up, blood pouring from the gash on his forehead. He produced a lopsided grin. "We have to stop meeting like this,"

"Oh, God, Ben, I'm so sorry." Carol knelt beside him, reached into her pocket, and pulled out a crumpled tissue. "This won't do. I need a towel."

"Kitchen. There's a drawer on the right hand side of the sink. I'd get it but I don't want to bleed all over my floor." He smiled again, blue eyes brilliant in his tanned face. "I just mopped it."

"Yes, okay." She nodded. "Right hand drawer. Got it. I'll be right back. Don't move, Ben. You might be hurt more than you realize."

"You worry too much."

His soft laughter followed her into his spotless kitchen. The pristine granite counter held a designer coffee pot, and his cup and saucer, nothing more, the beautiful china he used the day they met. She opened the drawer, smiling at the perfectly folded and stacked towels. Not an edge out of place. Talk about Type A personalities.

Suddenly, the floor shifted beneath her. She staggered. A chipped saucer bordered with flowers; a saucer holding a stump of candle … Her knees buckled. She grabbed the counter for support. Breathe, she commanded her lungs.

The image that had teased and eluded her since she discovered the bodies emerged with devastating clarity. Through her shock, she heard the screen door open and close.

"Having trouble finding a towel, Carol?"

She forced herself to turn. "No," she managed. "Here." She held out the towel. "Sorry. The sight of all that blood..." She shivered. "Dizzy."

He closed the space between them and took the towel from her outstretched hand.

"Maybe you should see a doctor, Ben. I think you need stitches." She tried to stem the panic that threatened to overtake her.

"Nah," he said, holding the folded towel to the cut, burying one bright blue eye behind it. "Get this bleeding stopped and a bandage will do the trick. I've had worse." The corner of his mouth lifted in a wry smile. "One year some neophyte cast his fly with great imprecision and hooked me in the eyelid. Now that hurt." He grinned, revealing a smear of blood on his front teeth.

Black dots danced at the edge of her vision.

"Carol." Ben's voice. Distant at first, now too loud. "Carol!"

She blinked, found her voice. "I need fresh air, Ben. The blood. I need to get outside." She moved to get past him, but he moved with her, blocking the door.

# 67

"Don't ever play poker." His visible eye rested on her, as empty of feeling as a shard of glass. His gaze went past her to the cup and saucer on the counter. "If I'd known you were coming I would have put my dishes away."

Carol attempted to dodge around him. If she could just get outside.

He moved with her, still talking. "Dumb, leaving that saucer behind. I should have thrown it away after Luce broke the cup, but it seemed fitting, somehow." He tossed the bloody towel into the sink without taking his eyes from her. A single drop of blood slid down his cheek and fell to the immaculate floor.

"Why?" Carol asked. "They thought the world of you, Ben. We all did."

"Because they deserved it. Luce was determined to return to her old life, even if it meant disobeying the judge's order and risking her chance to regain custody of her sons. She walked here after Jackson rescued her from that meth head. Came in the back way like she used to when we..." he faltered. "She came to say goodbye," he said, regaining his voice. "She told me Will was taking her back to Portland over the weekend." A nerve jumped in his jaw. "We had a thing for awhile, nothing serious. Scratching an itch you might say. Started not long after she got here. No one knew, least of all Will. She broke it off." His mouth twisted in nothing resembling a grin. "By then she'd told me about her sons, how she had no choice but to come to Winter." He dabbed at his forehead, studied the blood on the towel. "She had a responsibility to those kids, to take care of them, to be a good mother. So what does she do? She decides to take off before her probation's up, risks everything just so she can get back to her old life, running with the wrong crowd, leaving her kids in a foster home while she works in a bar, flirting with strangers."

He no longer resembled the man she knew. His eyes were fevered. The force of his rage sucked all the air from the room. She had to keep him talking, had to find a moment when she could get around him and out the door. God, why hadn't she called Will before she left the house? She forced herself to relax, to appear calm. "But Sarah. What did Sarah do?"

"Sweet Sarah." He pressed two fingers to his temple, studied the blood that stained them as though seeing it for the first time. "I thought Sarah was different. All she ever talked about was that son of hers, yet she was ready to forget about him if it meant spending more time with Dave. She claimed she was staying for school, but I knew better. All anyone had to do was look at those two to know what was going on in her mind."

His eyes returned to her. Carol thought they held regret.

"Mothers are supposed to act like mothers. Mothers don't leave little children all alone." The timbre of Ben's voice changed; became higher, child-like. "They don't leave them at the movies and forget to come after them. They don't bring mean men home who hurt them. They don't hit them for wetting their pants, or slap them when they touch her pretty blue dress."

"Is that what your mother did, Ben?"

His hands shot out and grabbed her shoulders. "You want to know what my mother did, Carol? You want to see? I'll show you." He spun her around and propelled her toward the stairs. She struggled against him as he pushed her up the steps, but that only caused her to stumble, and he showed no mercy in keeping her on her feet. When they reached the landing he held her by one arm and dragged her down a narrow hallway.

Carol glimpsed an open door, a neatly made bed.

He stopped at second door, bolted from the outside. Bolted, Carol realized with rising terror, to keep anyone from getting out. She tried to wrench free, kicked her foot back, and connected with his leg. It wasn't enough. Ben's iron grip on her neck didn't lessen. He slid the bolt back and with his hand on her neck, shoved her inside.

# 68

Carol locked her knees to keep from being forced into the room, but Ben's bruising hands overwhelmed her futile attempt. She gritted her teeth to stop their chattering. This was a nightmare. She'd wake any minute and Lady would jump on the bed to comfort her. But she wasn't dreaming. The nightmare was real. She saw the room by degrees, the slanted walls because this had once been an attic, blinds at two windows, both down, a spot of light escaping through a tear in one. A double bed pushed against the tallest wall, covered with – oh God, covered with plastic. Objects appeared as though viewed through water: a bedside table, a blue lamp, a humpbacked metal trunk. Ordinary objects in an ordinary room. Except for the smell. A miasma of pain and terror, blood and rot, weighted the air like a shroud, coated the inside of her mouth, her tongue, the back of her throat. She gagged. This was no bedroom. This was an abattoir.

Ben pushed her forward until she faced a wall. Taped newspaper clippings nearly covered it.

"Read." His voice harsh, his hands tight on her upper arms.

While her mind scrambled for a way to escape, she scanned the clippings, an honor roll of horrors: Baby Duct-taped to Crib by Mother's Boyfriend Dies of Starvation; Ten-year-old Boy Dies after Being Set on Fire by Mother's Ex-boyfriend; Missing Girl's Badly Beaten Body Found in Shallow Grave, Mother's Boyfriend Confesses. Some were accompanied by photographs, in one a blond haired child of two or three dressed in a Halloween costume to resemble a tiger, later found in the trunk of a car, beaten to death for wetting the bed. Another of a little girl, seven, maybe eight, taken at school. She sat unsmiling, dark hair uncombed, dark eyes turned inward, the plea in them unnoticed until her body was found buried in a California desert. Ben dragged her to another wall. More clippings, many yellow with age, all of children beaten, burned, starved, raped, tortured, murdered, tossed aside. "Here's the heart of my collection." He positioned her in front of a framed and glass-covered clipping that hung in the center. His breath blew hot against the side of her face.

"I'll read it to you. 'Called in the early hours of morning by a neighbor who reported screams coming from the house next door, police discovered Alec Wilkinson, age five, comatose and bleeding from a head wound. The fate of little Alec remains unknown at this time, although the same neighbor who called the police told this reporter the boy appeared dead when brought from the home. An older child was seen at Mercy Hospital before being released to Children's Services. An investigation is pending.'"

Carol fought to remain calm but the tremor in her voice wouldn't be stilled. "I don't understand. Why are you showing me this?"

If she could get him talking, get him to relax his grip, if only for a moment. "Did you know the Wilkinson's? Were you related?"

"Wilkinson was my name then." Ben said. "I changed it."

"But you told me you were an only child the day we met."

"I lied." He took his hands from her shoulders and reached to straighten the clipping frame.

The moment she'd prayed for. Carol ducked around him and ran. She made it from the bedroom, through the hall, raced down the stairs, taking two, and even three, at a time, her hand sliding down the railing, her breath whistling through her lips. Or was that Ben's breath she heard, closing fast behind her? Somehow, she managed to stay ahead, into the kitchen, through the door. If she could only reach the road.... She forgot about the ladder in the grass. The side rail caught her foot and sent her sprawling. Ben's weight pinned her to the ground. He flipped her onto her back. His hands went to her throat.

"Damn it, Carol, I didn't want this. I swear to God, I didn't."

Carol struck at his arms, clawed at him. No use. She scrabbled on the grass, her hands searching for a rock, a dirt clod, a tree branch, anything to break his grip on her neck. Ben's hands tightened. Her arms flailed. Her hand struck something hard.

Ben leaned down until his lips almost touched hers. "I'm sorry."

Carol held tight to the thing she held and swung upward, hitting Ben in the side of the neck.

"Jesus." He whispered the name like a prayer. His hands went to his neck. She watched him bring them away, staring in disbelief at the crimson rivulets that ran down his arms. She saw the jagged tear she'd opened there.

Then she realized. She'd struck him with his pruning saw, dropped when he fell from the ladder.

Ben smiled. The smile of the old Ben, the one she thought she knew. The man who tucked coffee beans into her grocery bag, and passed out licorice whips and bubble kits to children. His hand went back to his throat before his weight lifted from her body. Once on his feet, he took off across his yard, staggering toward the trees. Dry-mouthed and shaking, Carol rose and followed. She had to see this to the end. She owed Luce and Sarah that much.

How did he stay upright? The blood...

\*\*\*

Ben laughs, hearing the tell-tale rattle in his throat. Who would have believed she had it in her? His hands stay clamped against his neck where blood, slick as silk, slides through his fingers with stubborn persistence. The river, he wants the river. Water washes away sin, or so he was told long ago. Familiar voices clamor in his head. The one he knows best begs, "Sing me, Ben, sing me." His breath sounds wet to his ears. Hush little baby now don't you cry. He careens through the trees, reaches the river, and stumbles down the rocky slope and into the water's liquid embrace. The river floats him downstream. He sees his mother's face in the robin's-egg sky, Alec's tiny fingers curling around his own. Pushed by the current toward the river's center, his face slips beneath the surface. The world above is luminous, a shimmering landscape of color, like the Mother's Day card he made at school, saved in a drawer for a day that never came: blue paper and silver glitter that sparkled like the earrings she loved to wear. He sees her face, swollen with drink, the way her hands flew up like startled birds when he pressed his hands over her face. Alec's brilliant blue eyes, so like his own, follow him while the forgiving river carries him past smooth boulders, over a pearly cascade, and finally, wedges him deep and safe beneath a rocky ledge. Alec's tremulous voice, high and sweet, calls to him through the iridescent bubbles that rise through the gleaming water ... Alec ...

# 69

Will drove by the store, hit the brakes, and swore. Carol's bike. He'd been trying her on his cell phone until he hit Cayuse and lost service, his worry growing with every unanswered call, and all this time she'd been with Ben.

Relief warred with anger.

She didn't know it yet, but she was about to get a piece of his mind.

He cut a U-turn and pulled into the gravel lot. "Stay, Lady," he said, getting out of the truck. But she paid no attention, leaping through the door before he shut it and racing around to the back of the store.

Damn! Two women with minds of their own.

Will spotted the *Closed* sign on his way up the steps. He leaned his forehead against the window, cupped his hands around his eyes, and peered inside. No lights. Gone fishing? Taking Carol with him? In spite of his irritation, the thought made him smile.

Lady's insistent barking was getting on his nerves. She'd barked like that when Malone – *Christ!* Will ran toward the sound, his pulse kicking up. He reached the back yard and halted in mid-stride, shocked into stillness by sight of Carol, standing near a tree, eyes unblinking, face, clothing, even her hair, matted with blood. Lady stood beside her, no longer barking now that he had come.

"I'm not hurt, Will," she said, her voice holding the slightest tremor. "The blood is Ben's."

"Ben?" Had Malone shown in Winter after all, spotted Carol here, gone through Ben to get at her? "Where is Ben? Did Malone –"

"Ben's in the river," she said. "He killed Luce and Sarah. He tried to kill me." She pushed a bloodied strand of hair from her face, rubbed her hand against her jeans. "I killed him. With that." She pointed down. A pruning saw lay near her feet, the edge tacky with dark matter. Sounding more normal now, she came toward him. "I'll explain later. We need to go home. I have to call the sheriff."

# 70

Sheriff McReady put the phone down, more shocked than he cared to admit. Ben a killer? Carol killing Ben? He took a deep breath, picked up the phone again and contacted the tribal paramedics. They were closest and knew all the roads through the canyon. Even though she claimed she was fine, he wanted Carol checked over. Next, he called the tribal police and asked for assistance in finding Ben, whom she said had been carried away by the river. Baldwin, working double shifts in Dave's absence, had gone home earlier for some much needed rest but McReady hesitated for only a second before calling him. The deputy would want to be involved in this.

Jessica Washines and John Smartlowit reached the store moments after McReady. Smartlowit, in his forties with the lean body of a long-distance runner, climbed from the passenger side, his uniform crisp and sharply creased in spite of sitting strapped into the seat of the cruiser. Washines followed. The sheriff knew her best. Not yet out of her twenties, she'd gone to college on a basketball scholarship, got her degree and come home to join the police. She wore her hair coiled and pinned to the back of her head, but he'd seen her at Longhouse celebrations when she had it braided and wrapped with furs, watched her dance in her great-great grandmother's beaded buckskin dress, moving with effortless grace around the floor, feet stepping in time with the drum. She knew Sarah and the Blue Hawks, had volunteered countless off-duty hours in the search for her friend, and was devastated when Sarah's body was found.

The three shook hands, in no mood for talk.

Baldwin arrived, his bloodshot eyes testifying to lack of sleep. Together, they proceeded to the back of the store.

The ladder and pruning saw lay as Carol described them.

Baldwin bit his lip. "I still can't believe this," he said. "Ben?"

His confusion mirrored McReady's own. None of this made sense. He and Ben had fished together. Over countless cups of coffee they had carried on a good-natured, long-standing argument about the best dry fly to use for speckled trout.

Washines and Smartlowit set off on toward the river. McReady checked his pocket for the digital camera before he and Baldwin slipped on latex gloves. When they entered through the still-open back door, they stepped around spots of blood congealed on the floor. The cup and saucer Carol mentioned remained on the counter. The still-open drawer revealed neatly folded dishtowels. McReady snapped pictures of everything, including a shot of the stairs before they started up.

They passed the first bedroom, continued through the hall until they came to the second. McReady's scalp crawled at sight of the bolt outside the door. A faint but pervasive odor came from the room, slightly sweet yet tinged with rot, like fruit left out too long.

He snapped pictures of the bed, bedside table, trunk, and clippings on the walls. A single closet opened on emptiness. He checked the connecting bathroom. Spotless basin, tub, and toilet; jugs of bleach in the cupboard beneath the basin along with bottles of foaming bath oil: Lily of the Valley, Lavender, Wild Rose. Bile rose in his throat. He forced it back, kept taking pictures, returning to the bed room in time to hear Baldwin's anguished, "Oh, Jesus." The deputy held an open jewelry case in his hands, inside a collection of mismatched earrings.

"Souvenirs," he whispered.

McReady snapped a picture, told Baldwin to close the case and put it back in the drawer. He turned to the trunk. Unlocked. He hoped that meant empty. It didn't. The first thing to catch his eye, a much-folded piece of paper maybe four inches square. He photographed it before unfolding. His breath caught. A map. Tiny crosses scattered across its face. Their significance hit him like a roundhouse punch to his gut.

His horror growing, McReady begin lifting a succession of garments from the trunk. Women's clothing, laundered, ironed, and neatly folded before storing away. He remembered his sister wearing an outfit much like one near the bottom, a style popular at that time. That had been twenty years ago. Dear God, how long had this been going on?

He replaced everything as he'd found it, and closed the lid, his thoughts swirling. As sheriff, he had arrested people for many reasons, wife-beating, vandalism, theft. He had helped cut teenage bodies from the twisted wreckage of cars and dealt with lonely people who fabricated complaints just to have someone to talk to. He was not a young man, nor did he consider himself a naïve one. But this? This surpassed all understanding. How could the Ben Wagner he knew, the man everyone in Winter knew, whose store was a gathering place for neighbors, the man who made children laugh, and traded outrageous fishing stories with anyone who'd listen, how could that Ben Wagner be the monster revealed by this room?

A low groan came from Baldwin. The deputy was reading one of the clippings, his face waxy, without color. Was he about to pass out or throw up?

"Let's get out of here," the sheriff said, clapping the young man on the shoulder. "We both need a dose of fresh air."

\*\*\*

While McReady and Baldwin searched Ben's dwelling, Washines and Smartlowit followed his erratic blood trail to the river. They broke from the trees onto the river bank; saw more blood on the rocks leading to the water's edge. After walking downstream for a mile without sighting his body, they returned to their cruiser and radioed for additional manpower.

\*\*\*

Jim Olney discovered the body half in, half out of the river near the Cayuse Bridge, several miles downstream. Long familiar with the ways of the Umatilla, he'd suspected as much and came to check while others poled rapids and deep water pools between Cayuse and the store.

# 71

After the autopsy, Ben's body was released for burial, a grim affair made more so by the media who showed up in force to record every moment. This time there were no flowers. The grave itself lay in a far corner, as though even in death, Ben posed a threat.

Carol didn't hate him. As the story of his life unfolded she saw a child who'd lost everything, mother, brother, home, in a single evening. But Luce had suffered an equally tragic childhood. She hadn't taken her anger out on innocents. Ben chose to play God, killing women he judged unfit as mothers; that much she'd gleaned from his rant in that terrible room. He'd shown no concern for the children left behind, many forced into state care as he had been. In a way, he seemed to be punishing them too.

\*\*\*

That evening, Will uncorked a bottle of wine while she set the table.

"Looks wonderful," he said of the pot roast and vegetables. He kissed her gently on the cheek before they sat down.

Carol was pouring gravy over her mashed potatoes when footsteps drummed on the porch, followed by a hard knock at the door. Will pushed back from the table. "I'll get it."

She heard snatches of conversation that made no sense before the door shut and the footsteps receded. Will returned, placed his hands on her shoulders.

"The store's on fire."

\*\*\*

He parked well behind the fire line, gave her a quick kiss before he jumped out and hurried to Jackson and Rick, wielding the water hose. Carol let herself out of the pickup and stared at the nightmarish scene. Flames licked the sky. Black smoke shot through with fiery sparks, boiled from the old wooden structure. Volunteers worked to keep the fire from spreading. With nothing more than a pump truck, containment was the best they could hope for. In all that frenzied movement, the unnatural stillness of one man caught her eye. Dave. Standing too near the flames. In the blazing light he appeared carved from stone, and Carol wondered that no one else noticed. She walked slowly toward him, warned by his stance to approach with caution. Heat from the fire seared her skin. Dave acted immune to it. When she drew nearer, she saw two red gas containers at his feet. She looked back over her shoulder, searching for Will. He must have sensed her need because he turned and scanned the crowd until he found her.

She pointed to Dave. Will mouthed a few words to Jackson and jogged over.

"Stay here, I'll get him." Will walked to Dave, put himself between him and the fire. She couldn't hear what he said over the roar of the flames, but his words had no effect. Dave, impassive, stared ahead, lost in his own private hell. When Will reached for his arm, Dave shrugged him off.

Carol joined the two. Together, she and Will managed to lead Dave into the hands of the paramedics.

"Shock," said one, assessing Dave's blind stare. "We'll take it from here."

He and his partner got Dave into the back of the ambulance, placed him on a cot and covered him with blankets before belting him in.

"I'm going with him." Will's tone brooked no argument.

"Okay then," the second medic said. "Let's roll."

"Keys are in the pickup, Carol," Will said. "I'll see you at the hospital."

An explosion rocked the remains of the building as the ambulance disappeared from sight. More black smoke rose from the rubble, plunging day into night. When it cleared, Rick's voice rang out. He pointed toward the river where a column of flame and smoke rose above the trees. The house where she found Luce and Sarah, Carol realized. Dave had torched it, too. She thought of the brush stacked against the door, the trees and blackberry vines that surrounded the place, and jumped when someone nudged her.

"See what lightning can do?" Lorrie gazed at the rubble, her voice calm, matter-of-fact. "Summer thunderstorms are a real danger here."

Carol understood. Dave hadn't set the fires. Dave was no where near when lightning struck. The gas containers, she saw now, were gone. She could live with that. In fact, if she had her way, she'd cover what was left of both places with salt for good measure.

"Yes," she said, slipping her arm through Lorrie's. "They are."

The canyon protected its own.

# 72

A week after the fire, Carol visited the cemetery. Thunder clouds were building over the hills, the tang of ozone heavy in the air. A true summer storm was on the way, bringing wind and blowing dust before the cooling rain. She placed a bouquet of red and gold nasturtiums, purple butterfly bush, and bright yellow sunflowers at the base of the headstone. Later, as the seasons turned, she'd bring autumn leaves, rose hips, and sprigs of pine. One day Luce's children would visit their mother's grave. Carol wanted them to see that she wasn't forgotten. She wished she could leave flowers for Sarah, but Sarah would remain in her heart forever, as she would in Dave's, and everyone who knew her.

She and Will had visited Dave the day before. Tragedy had etched new lines in his young face, and his voice no longer held the exuberance it once had, but his eyes were clear and his hands steady as he talked about Sarah. The only time his voice clogged with unshed tears was when he described how her son, Brandon, kept asking why momma didn't wake up to play with him.

A stiff breeze whipped through the cemetery, tossing the crowns on the trees, scattering leaves and faded white Locust blossoms into the barren field beyond the fence.

Almost against her will, her gaze roamed to the corner grave. The earth over Ben had settled; the river rocks that ringed it looked dull away from the water that gave them life. She sometimes dreamed of that moment in his yard when he tried to kill her, the way he smiled after she struck him. He'd almost looked relieved.

Branches creaked in the strengthening wind. Carol touched her fingers to Luce's headstone, turned to go and saw Will coming through the gate. In the storm's gathering darkness, he seemed more shadow than substance, and for a moment Carol believed her eyes were playing tricks. He must have noticed her leaving with the flowers and guessed what she had in mind.

She had never found the right moment to tell him what really happened that day on the creek. Her last secret, one she'd kept the true meaning of even from herself. What better place than a cemetery to lay it to rest?

He reached her as the first drops of rain spattered the earth around them. She fixed her eyes on his and drew in a deep breath. She let it out, and the past with it.

"That day we..." she stopped, swallowed. "That day at the creek, when Ray found us." Her hands fell to her sides. She backed away from him. "Ray raped me. He said he'd kill you if I told anyone. I was pregnant when I left Winter. That's why my mother destroyed the letters. She blamed everyone; my uncle, my friends, but most of all, you."

Confusion warred with denial before understanding came. Will's eyes darkened with hurt. Carol almost regretted telling him – almost. But keeping that secret had affected her entire life. She didn't want to carry it any longer. Will deserved the truth. All of it.

"You were protecting me," he said, wonder in his voice. "You went through that alone to keep me safe."

"At first, yes. But later? I could have made it right, but I was angry. I thought you forgot about me, that you didn't care. I wanted to get even, let my family blame you. Uncle James died believing you were responsible. James, the one person beside your mom who had been good to you, whom you cared for. I'm so sorry."

The rain started in earnest, rivulets streaking their faces.

Will shook his head, his eyes never leaving her. "My God, Carol, you were fifteen. Stop beating yourself up. What you must have gone through, on you own, makes me so sad. How could you think I'd blame you now?" He stepped forward; erasing the distance between them. "We've both made mistakes, I think I told you that once before. Who hasn't?" He reached out, smoothed her hair with his hand. "Who was it that said the past is gone, today is a gift, that's why it's called the present?"

"I don't know."

"Smart person, whoever it was." He leaned down and kissed the tip of her nose. "Now let's go home before we both drown."

# EPILOGUE

**M**aples and sycamores, ancient lilac bushes and dogwoods dot the sloping, emerald-colored grounds. The maples are turning, their leaves smoke and topaz, ruby and peridot. In spite of an overcast sky, the day is pleasant, the colors of autumn more pronounced beneath the soft gray clouds.

The state institution in Salem resembles a college. Faded brick buildings hold the light and seem to glow from within. Ivy covers many of the walls. Small groups of people walk together on paths shaded by overarching sycamore branches. From a distance, they seem like students and mentors instead of patients and caregivers.

On a wrought iron bench, a man fastens startling blue eyes on a chipmunk. A happy smile creases his face, softening the grotesque shape of his skull, flattened on one side and devoid of hair. Wispy white strands sprout from it, forming a lopsided halo that lends him the appearance of a drunken saint. He brings his hands together in a soft clap, and the chipmunk scurries closer.

"Good morning, Alec, enjoying the fall day? I think the sun's about to break through." The speaker, dressed in white, has long, dark hair gathered in a ponytail at the back of his neck. A nametag on his shirt pocket reads: Greg Collins, Caregiver. "How about a peanut for your friend, Alec?" Greg reaches into his pocket and brings out peanuts in their shells. "Here you go, give the little guy his treat."

Alec's smile is beatific. "Thank you, Ben."

His words are slurred, halting, like a record played at the wrong speed.

Greg is used to being called Ben. Alec calls everyone Ben, even his female attendants.

"We're not sure why," one supervisor said, when Greg, newly arrived, asked about it. "Most likely, the name became trapped in his mind at the time of his accident. He was only five, you know."

And now, he's five forever, Collins thinks.

An impatient churr comes from the expectant chipmunk.

"Now, Ben?"

"Yes, Alec. Now."

Alec leans forward, hand outstretched. The chipmunk grasps the peanut between its paws before he scurries up Alec's arm to his shoulder, where he proceeds to shell and eat his treat.

The sun breaks through the clouds.

Alec's delighted laughter echoes through the stately grounds. "Look, Ben! He likes me!"

His unabashed joy brings a lump to Collins' throat.

Every day that weather allows, Alec feeds the chipmunk, yet each morning he is as thrilled by the animal's attention as he was the day before, and the day before that. Alec's world lies outside of time. It has no past or future. Tomorrow he will be as excited as he is today, as he was yesterday and all the days before. In a way, Greg thinks this is a good thing.

"Yes, he does, Alec. He surely does."

But Alec's attention has already drifted back to the small creature perched on his lap. One atrophied hand gently strokes the fur between the animal's ears. He begins to hum, then to sing in his dragging, rust-coated voice. The melody is off-key and the words almost too garbled to comprehend, but Greg, himself a father, recognizes the lullaby, one his wife often sings to their little girl at bedtime.

"Hush little baby, don't you cry..."

## *The End*

# Acknowledgments

Thanks to Cathy Burleson and Carrie Bremer for reading early drafts of Winter; to the Internet Writers Workshop whose novel group guided me forward to the next draft, to Antoinette Kennedy for her painstaking review and editing, Barbara J. Taylor for an additional look-through, and to Sarah Woodbury, Ph.D. for sharing her time and wisdom in getting this to print.

Any errors are mine alone.

# About the Author

Judith Kelly Quaempts is a poet and novelist. She was born in Oregon but raised on Air Force bases in several states, including Hawaii and Alaska. She's worked as an x-ray technician, a medical secretary, a police 'matron,' and as an executive assistant in the science and technology division of a DC lobbying association. She currently resides in Athena, a small city in rural eastern Oregon.

Printed in Great Britain
by Amazon